THE
KRAKEN SEA

THE KRAKEN SEA

E. CATHERINE TOBLER

APEX PUBLICATIONS
LEXINGTON, KY

The Kraken Sea © 2016 by E. Catherine Tobler.

ISBN: 978-1-937009-40-3

Cover Art © Magdalena Pągowska
Title Design by Mekenzie Larsen
Edited by Jason Sizemore

Published by Apex Publications, LLC
PO Box 24323
Lexington, KY 40524

First Edition: June, 2016

Visit us at www.apexbookcompany.com

To all who wish to find a place they will fit.

It began with a dragon in the pouring rain, the beast barely held at bay, balanced upon two thin steel rails. Steam poured from its black mouth and guts, billowing through the damp gloom. A brief spark of after-rain sunlight caught within its glassy green eye, against sharp metal tooth, and when the steam gave way, young Jackson could see it was no dragon, but a train. The train was headed as far west as it could go and Jackson, aged fifteen-and-one-half, in the Year of Our Lord 1893, would be on it.

The ill-fitting wool coat wrapping him hung to his knees, gray sleeves rucked to his elbows. The coat's wide collar served as a perch for the pinned paper bearing his name (lifted from a box of discarded daffodils in an alley) and his pedigree (none). No parent had given him his name, that party having only the decency to leave him in the box, partly sheltering him from the snow of a winter's night. The much-worn box sat on a shelf in the foundling hospital, filled with penny dreadfuls above the narrow, squeaky bed Jackson had once occupied.

Jackson served as first and last name both, the nuns never having time to decide which it was and provide another. Other children suggested "Francis," for his affinity with the rooftop pigeons. Jackson corrected them at every opportunity, be it with words or fists or solid shoe heels. He liked Saint Francis well enough, but it was not his name.

The nuns ensured he had three meals a day and shoes on his feet, even when every week these things became an increasing challenge. But the nuns told him someone was waiting for him in San Francisco — someone who had asked for a boy of his kind. A boy who was brown-haired and strong, a boy who was not afraid of water. Jackson didn't know anyone in San Francisco, hardly knew anyone in New York, but it didn't matter. It didn't matter he was the oldest of the group, that those who had come to the foundling hospital with him were long gone. It didn't matter that no family had wanted him before now. The train mattered.

The sisters nudged him up the steps into the passenger car. His fingers moved over the green velveteen seats, polished boots thumping on the faded violet carpet between the seats. Other children already packed those seats, wrapped in coats similar to his, names pinned to collars. Their faces were all the same to him, wide-eyed, lips near chewed to bloodiness because they were so worried.

He became aware of Sister Jerome Grace's absence then, even if he thought he could hear her voice. She had not been chosen to join the orphan train across the country. He pictured her soft hand in his as he walked to the end of the car and crawled onto an empty bench near a window where he could look out at the people who bustled through the station. Where he could look at —

"Sister Jerome Grace?"

Her face tipped up, smiling at him from the platform. He imagined her hair was dark, though he had never seen it for the veil she wore, eyebrows the indiscriminate color of shadows hastily dropped. Rain pearled on her veil now, transforming the flat black fabric into a field of diamonds. When the sister walked toward the train, the rain slid off in a crystal curtain that hovered in the humid, fogged air. She was damp when she settled beside Jackson.

"A change of plans," was all she said, and smiled at him before beginning to count the children in the car and the sisters assigned to wrangle them. Her pale hand hovered in the air, her first finger pointing at each child counted, tallies made.

Sister Jerome Grace was twenty-five, married to God for always and ever. She had never told him the name she was born with. Jackson turned his flushed face back to the window, chewing the inside of his cheek much as those other children chewed their lips. He swallowed the blood when he tasted it. He pulled the cuffs of his coat down to make certain his arms were covered, even though the sister knew all there was to know about him. She would not be surprised by a gleam of scale even if it often terrified him. What was inside him that made him so?

When, at the shriek of the train's whistle, he stood up on the velveteen seat and cried out, he shuddered. It wasn't human, the sound the train whistle pulled from his guts. He sang a duet with the whistle, a high lingering note that said he was as ready as the train. Ready to go. Clear the tracks.

Sister Jerome Grace's voice reached him, but he couldn't answer her when she asked what was wrong. His mouth tightened up, tongue pressed to teeth. He knew the children were looking at him as though he were mad, but he was long-used to such looks.

One hand pressed to the window and the other pressed to his chest, where he could feel the resonating whistle. His fingers tensed against the window and when the whistle sounded a second time, he cried out again. It wasn't alarm, only utter joy. Who knew the beast had such a voice? The sound crawled inside him, deep down into his gut where nothing but Sister Jerome Grace had lodged before. Only her and now the dragon's call. His hand thumped against the window, leaving a smudge.

"Get down, Jackson. Ssstoppit!"

Someone tugged on the hem of his coat. Jackson smacked the hand away and it never came again. By the time the train pulled out of the station, Jackson had the length of bench to himself but for Sister Jerome Grace. When Sister Mary Luke suggested other children spread out and join Jackson, they shook their heads. He was oldest; he was strangest.

A little girl thrashed in Sister Mary Luke's grip when the nun attempted to move her, throwing herself to the floor rather than sit beside Jackson. He watched, impassive, content with Sister Jerome Grace nearby and the rumble of the train in his bones. His hand stayed pressed to the window as the city retreated into his past.

His past was a place he didn't know well, but a place the sisters had always speculated about. They told him he'd come to the foundling hospital as many children did, a tiny thing inside a tiny box. "A Christmas gift," Jackson had said, making the sisters laugh. None of them minded the gift of him, even though it was another body to clothe, another mouth to feed.

The rain returned outside the window, so Jackson turned his attention to the other children. He watched the way they spoke to one another, the way two heads bent together over a shared book, the way they poked and teased when the sisters were outside of earshot or arm reach. It was peculiar to him, friendship; he hadn't made peace with himself and couldn't see how to make it with anyone else Jackson missed the pigeons and their aviary on the roof, though Sister Jerome Grace promised San Francisco had birds.

The sleeping compartments were small and narrow. Jackson vanished into his without complaint when the time came, wondering if it was because the space resembled that long-ago daffodil box. The sisters told him he couldn't possibly remember the box, but he knew its neatly made walls, smooth wood to keep tender blossoms from bruising in transit. Only Sister Jerome Grace asked him about it. It was cold that night, he'd told her. The first snow of the season, and she said yes, yes, remembering too. He disliked being cold even now.

"How long will it take us?" he asked the next day, the train continuing along endless tracks. The country spooled out along side them, always changing. Houses gave way to cities that gave way to plains until there were more houses, more cities. The buildings fascinated him, in hues of brown and sepia, ivory and black.

"Just over a week."

The sister's answer was thrilling and disappointing both. Being on the train for an entire week was something he meant to take advantage of. He wanted to learn its ways — her ways — how she was put together, how she moved over the rails. But disappointment was quick to follow. It was only a week and part of him wanted to stay on the train wherever she might go, even if she only snaked back and forth over the same east-west track.

It was with relief he discovered there would be stops along the way. Sister Jerome Grace offered him the map of the rails before she vanished in a flurry of black skirts to chase after a pair of children who had broken Sister Mary Luke's rosary.

The journey and its many pauses made sense, train depots and cities scattered along the way. Refueling, taking on more food. Jackson traced the lines on the map with careful fingers, realizing not all of the children would reach the coast with him, having been chosen by families closer than San Francisco.

Families who had asked for them.

He turned the map over then looked to his reflection in the train's window. A common boy at first glance, he imagined his paperwork said; do not be alarmed by the discoloration of his skin, nor the way he may shed. Surely his papers said no such thing, and yet. A finger strayed to his wrist, rubbing until he saw an iridescent gleam where his pulse beat.

"Jackson."

He looked at the sister, allowing her to take his hand and examine both fingertip and wrist. Her hands were warm from running after children. Jackson's wrist gleamed with scale, a snakeskin pattern revealed. He thought hard about unbroken skin and slowly his own settled back to ordinary flesh. Sometimes control came easily, though he could not say why. He suspected Sister Jerome Grace was of help. She had never shied over his strangeness and that was a comfort.

"There is a place I want to show you in Chicago," she said and eased her hold on him. She lifted the map from where it had fallen and turned it to the side containing the train's stops. "Here." She touched a city resting against the edge of a large lake.

"What place?" Jackson asked. Every place outside the windows called to him.

"We will have an afternoon there, and you will see."

If the train had given Jackson cause to shout, Chicago gave him cause to gape. Sister Jerome Grace said they called it the White City, but everything bled red around the edges for him — red with blood and life. He was a young man of books and lessons, of a life lived within specific confines, and to see things he had only read about had a way of stealing his speech. He disliked this reaction, but couldn't force himself to speak. The hospital yard had been his chief exposure to grass and living things, the hospital roof where he learned the sky with its clouds and stars, and that other places lay beyond what confined him. He would count the buildings while feeding the pigeons, but never came to count them all. It was the same with Chicago and the Colombian Exposition.

It was called a world's fair and devastation flooded Jackson at the sight of its marvels. They would have the afternoon, the sisters said, but no more because the train was scheduled to leave. Jackson knew there was more to this place than could be discovered in a few scant hours. Two children were united with their foster parents at the train station and Jackson's throat closed tight when those same parents told the kids the fair would be there through October. There was plenty of time.

How time could be both in abundance and such dire need confused Jackson. Much as he found himself able to shut the strangest parts of himself away because they frightened him too much, he buttoned up the con-

fusion too. The fair soon had its way with him, no matter that his slight
time would be spent with a group of nuns and children he stood heads
above. The children ignored him, as they always had, so Jackson soaked in
everything else.

The Ferris wheel against the sky reinforced how small Jackson felt
outside the hospital walls. Watching the wheel disgorge people from its
enclosed cars confirmed any one of them might be swallowed by something larger at any moment. It solidified his belief that the world was full
of larger monsters than he — what was a little bit of snakeskin in the face
of such a place as this? When he and the sisters and children piled into a
windowed car to ride the wheel up and around, he held his breath, half
thinking they would be flung into the clouds. He didn't fear such a thing,
but rather welcomed it, until he saw Sister Jerome Grace's face.

"I never even go onto the roof of the hospital," she whispered. Her
hands curled around the rail encircling the car's interior until her nails
gleamed white at the edges.

"It's not so awful." He noticed the way she had trouble even looking
out the windows as the car rose. "Look forward, not back." He turned her
as much as her grip on the rail would allow, so she might see the car rise
over the fair and into the sky. The sister floundered.

"And then just move with the car." As it lifted over the top of the wheel,
Jackson turned her again, but the car paused there, to give everyone a good
look at the fair spreading in every direction around them. It was its own
little city, wholly contained if ephemeral. Jackson supposed it was part of
the beauty; like the stars above the hospital on a clear night, it would be
lost, no matter that others had more leisure to explore it.

The children in the car jumped, which made it swing and the sisters
swoon. But Sister Jerome Grace smiled now and Jackson let go of her. She
turned when the car moved once more, so she could watch their descent

along the backside of the wheel.

"Would have been worse on a roof," Jackson said as they streamed from the car and the sister steadied herself with a hand on the door, as if she had been at sea for years. At her puzzled frown, his mouth split in a smile. "The roof doesn't move, but pigeons shit an awful lot."

Sister Jerome Grace laughed, a hand covering her mouth when Sisters Mary Luke and Roberta looked askance. The sister fell into line with the others and Jackson dropped to the back, to trail behind the way he often did in the hospital, knowing no one wanted to hold his hand and skip toward the next destination as they did with others. The children paired off as they had been taught, hands clasped while others pointed here and there.

Jackson's gaze wandered until it settled upon the striped canvas hanging near the great wheel. The canvas enclosed a hidden space and without a word to any of the sisters, Jackson made for it. Up close, the canvas was sloppy, red paint striped down fabric the color of old bone.

A trio of young ladies clad in ivory day dresses emerged from a flap in the canvas, two of them supporting one who had swooned. Jackson stared at them and they did not see him, so he took his time in looking. They were as strange to him as this place, older than any other girl he knew but for the sisters, and the sisters didn't count. Not in that way. The two girls dragged the third toward a log nearby and sat her down, fanning her face. She didn't seem inclined to rouse, chin bent to chest, dark brown curls brushing pale cheeks.

One of them saw him then. "Can you get her some water, please?"

Jackson stepped instead through the flap the girls had emerged from. Whatever lay inside the tent had a hold of him and he wouldn't be turned. He heard a hasty curse from the girls as the flap fell closed then a hand slid over his shoulder.

"Come in, come in."

The tent smelled like the paint used to stripe the canvas, but other scents mingled: dark earth, rot, wet. The man who welcomed him was a sight in a gold coat, crisp white shirt, and crimson vest beneath. A watch chain gleamed at his belly, a mustache curling over his smiling mouth. Jackson was not well acquainted with men outside the priests of the foundling hospital, but this man had an oily feel to him much as they did. He wanted to sell something, wanted a belief drawn into young hands for coddling.

"We've wonders to amaze and astonish, but if you've a delicate stomach, best go the way those young ladies did," the hawker warned.

Jackson's eyes narrowed. He couldn't imagine what they might have seen, but wanted to take his turn at it. "I'm no young lady," he said, and the man's smile deepened.

"Well then." The man stepped back and inclined his head, as if to say good day. Jackson turned, attention already elsewhere. Someone cried in alarm, but this didn't deter Jackson. It only made him more curious, silencing the normal voice of panic inside him.

More canvas inside the tent was suspended from the ceiling to create hallways and walls. This canvas was unpainted and smelled musty. Smelled of shit, too, as if perhaps it had once enclosed animals, though what animals Jackson could not venture to say, picturing only tame things such as horses.

He rounded a corner into the first small room and stared at the table in its center. Upon it stood a jar the size of a cask; the jar was filled with clouded liquid, a blooming flower suspended within. The flower was the color of a New York sunrise in summer before the day grew too warm. Jackson strode closer, to the table's edge where he crouched to get a better look.

He wondered if Alice knew this upon entering Wonderland, seeing everything she could not name. If, when she looked at one object, a flower, but abruptly realized it was something else. Not a thing grown in the ground, but rather a thing grown in a body.

The clouded liquid supported not a flower, but a small body. It was no larger than a newborn pup curled in on itself. But where a pup could only curl once, chin to chest much as the young lady outside, this form curled into itself countless times. Where its chin was, Jackson could not say, for it was lost in a froth of cold flesh. There was a tail, or perhaps it was an arm, because there were three perfectly formed fingers at its end.

Jackson's lips parted. He had no idea what it was, but could not look away. Sounds deeper in the tent eventually drew him on, another cry and a rustle as if someone had been caught before they could hit the ground.

There were twelve rooms in all and Jackson visited each, startled each time. The most startling, which was hard to quantify he decided later, was the woman in the cage. Her skin shone with the color of rotted green apples, bare hip and breast curving upward in shadow. She didn't have legs the way a normal woman must (Jackson had wondered, of course, what might be hidden under all skirts, perhaps it was this, ever this), but large, scaled viper coils slithering over the ground. Such coils were painfully familiar to him. He wriggled his feet in his tight-laced shoes as if to confirm he was holding his shape. He wouldn't let the beast out, he wouldn't.

Something awful lingered in her eyes, something else he recognized. That look of being found strange, of being both loved and hated for it, but mostly always hated. She slithered to the cage bars and wrapped her hands around the metal. She said nothing, but her misery was clear. Her eyes were shadowed now, but Jackson saw them clear as day. Clear as this entire tent, filled with things like him.

He had worked so long and hard to learn the ways of holding himself together. Some days were worse than others. Some days, the truth of him wanted to spill everywhere like flooding water. Other days he found it easy to assume this false shape to pass unseen. But in this warm tent, he began to spill. This was why they gave him up, he had told himself over and over as he tried to find sleep. This was why his parents tucked him into a wood box and left him on the hospital's back stoop. This was what hid inside of him, a creature that others would cage.

"Boy?"

The man and his mustache — Jackson could smell him now, oil amid the musk of the woman. But it was already too late; Jackson's hands were no longer hands. They had vanished into the cuffs of the coat he wore, wriggling in a thousand directions as crimson scale swallowed his ordinary skin. His tight-laced shoes burst open, ruined as leg-thick coils identical to the woman's slithered out. His trouser seams split to the knee and he made a great bellowing sound, like none he had before. His rage and fear poured out, careless, haphazard. The man and his mustache toppled backward, the woman in the cage rattling the door in a plea.

The door was little obstacle. Jackson flung one arm, enveloped two bars, and pulled. He threw the door, taking pleasure in the way it ripped through tent canvas and displays alike. He gave no thought to the others inside in the tent — was only vaguely aware of the distant shrieks as his attention rested on the man who had imprisoned Jackson's own kind.

Much as his appendages had coiled around the bars, they now closed around the hawker's throat. There was a burble, the sound before breath bleeds entirely away. Jackson eased his hold only slightly, because he wouldn't finish with this man so quickly. He wanted to see the fear in the man's eyes before he swallowed him. The hawker's head shook, eyes blown wide and terrified, Jackson's own true image reflected within. If Jackson had a proper mouth, he might have smiled, but his mouth was in no way proper. This gaping maw could only expand.

There was no scream, only a muffled groan Jackson swallowed. Screams came from others stampeding from the tent, from more tangled in the canvas. The scent of rotten liquids began to rise, jars and tanks broken, contents spilled. Old flesh and new began to dissolve in the air as Jackson came back to himself, as he began to dwindle from monster back to boy.

It was there he saw her first: the girl who had fainted and needed water. The tent had collapsed, allowing him to see the log where she had been taken. Her chin was no longer bent to her chest and her eyes —

Her eyes were black and on him. She did not look away.

Sister Jerome Grace found Jackson in the train yard, rocking back and forth in the late afternoon sun, clothes in tatters. His shoes were missing, feet whipping viper coils, and when she wasn't surprised, he wasn't surprised. They had been here before. She had asked him not to come back to this place, but this place was home, torn and imperfect, but his own no matter where else he might go.

"Breathe."

Jackson breathed, their positions reversed from what they had been in the wheel's windowed car. She was telling him, he knew, to go with the world and not against it, to ease the sickness wanting to swallow him. It was harder now.

It would happen more regularly with the onset of adulthood, the priests had speculated. He shouldn't be kept under a holy roof, they had often said. But crosses did not burn him nor did prayers send him running, so he was kept, he was believed in, he was given a place he was now being taken from. Taken and placed in a world he did not — could not — understand, and anger rushed up his spine, a flood of blood and rage.

"Jac —"

He seemed to step outside himself, watching as one thick arm lifted. It pushed Sister Jerome Grace back, flinging her to the ground like trash. The blackness, when it swallowed him, did not entirely carry him away, because he saw everything, felt everything. There was no escaping what had a hold of him. Jackson ran, deeper into the tangle of tracks and trains, but the sister's voice held him as she followed, and bid him come back.

"Tell me what I am!" Jackson's words were a ragged bellow from an imperfect mouth that wanted only to howl. He stayed a train car length ahead of her, not letting her catch him. The coils of his lower body whispered over the stones, the railroad ties, the steel tracks as he passed between parked trains. He had no control, as though everything he had learned within the foundling hospital's walls had been ripped away. This clear sky was too large, his own kind caged beneath it.

She said what they always said when he asked. "We don't know. Jackson —"

He moved like water, at the sister's side in an instant. One not-hand wrapped around her throat when before he had never dared touch her beyond her hands or sleeved arms. Beneath the fabric closing her away from the world, he could feel the hammer of her heart. Part of him wanted to draw back and not invade her space, but he stayed as he was. He pressed her into the side of the train car, feeling his body stretch taller, darker, a spreading stain.

"You have some idea." His voice was close to splintering and he drew a breath, forced some measure of stillness into himself. "Don't tell me what *they* think. Those men of God." He spat and closed his not-hand more tightly around her throat. "Tell me what *you* think. You, who have known me all these years. You, who have never told me the name your parents gave you."

Warmth flooded into Sister Jerome Grace's cheeks; Jackson could feel it sluice from her skin and he bit his cheek, forcing himself to give her time to answer. She did not look at him.

"We do not speak of these things," she said.

He expected her to whisper, to flounder, but that was gone from her. She did not try to wrest herself from his hold, only lifted her hand, to reveal her palm. Her other hand lifted her belt, adorned with the scapulars she wore, her rosary, and a small pair of silver scissors. It was the scissors she untangled, lifting their sharpened point to her exposed palm. She slashed down and into the lined skin before Jackson could think of stopping her.

He expected blood and for her to cry out. He heard only the rumble of an approaching train and there was no blood. The flesh of Sister Jerome Grace's palm split to reveal what looked like a thousand writhing snakes, but as they spilled out, he saw they were threads. They were colorless, yet glowed in the afternoon light. Each looked identical to the others, he could tell no difference between. They whispered through her fingers, never falling to the ground, but twining around fingers and wrists, and back into the opened flesh.

"You have read your mythology," the sister said, voice low, but he could hear her above the rumble of the train as it passed two tracks over.

One thread lifted from the mass, sliding around Jackson's own wrist and it never occurred to him to fear it because it was like his own scaled skin. He knew it for his own. His thread, inside the sister's palm.

"I know what you are. I made you what you are, before the world was as it is. Before humanity was in ruin."

As the thread tightened, Jackson saw a landscape unfold in his mind. Long rolling grasses spread under a sky too blue to look at long. In the far distance, white marble jutted against the sky, and he could smell a fire, a sacrifice. He moved through the field not as a man might but as a god would. He was snake and man both, perfectly fused.

"I spun your thread," she said, "and my sister could not bear to cut it — you have come to its end many times, but she splices it, ties it to another, and back you come."

"We have been here before?" His gaze stayed on her. He sensed the metal of the trains weighing on them both, keeping them anchored.

Sister Jerome Grace nodded only once. "Yes and no." Her eyes met his at long last, grave and nearly gray in the shadow of him. "You must go to San Francisco and be what you will."

Jackson tightened his hold on her neck, pushing her into the train car door. She did not protest — if they had been here before, she knew he would not hurt her. He knew this too, but doubted the courtesy could extend beyond this occasion. He stared, seeing in her eyes another figure, something he couldn't understand. A figure in a corner, a figure who said nothing, but only stared back.

"You spin threads and your sister cuts." One curling tentacle of a finger slid up her cheek and she did not blink, only watched him long and calm. He stroked the edge of her veil, the line of her temple. "There is a third." Three was holy — three was sacred. There were three Fates, this he knew as well as he knew anything he had ever read in a book.

"Yes."

Jackson drew into the false skin he showed to the world. Every strange part of him withered, became normal. He was nothing more than an ordinary boy when he got hold of himself, trousers tattered, but it was feet peeking out at him, ten normal toes grimed with the muck of the train yard.

The sister let her scissors drop into the folds of her black skirts and her hand knit itself back together, all the threads swallowed up into her as the seam closed without flaw. He wondered if spools would spill out should she be split down her middle. If under her veil it wasn't hair at all, but braided coils of colored thread, and he ached to know. How easy it would be, he thought, to pull that fabric loose.

Instead, he drew his chilled hands into the over-sized sleeves of his coat, and only followed her when she led the way back to the train. She ensured no one saw him as he made his way to the sleeping compartment, to find clothes whole and untorn.

Jackson's suitcase belonged to someone else before he owned it. Probably another orphan, the sister had told him, though even she claimed not to know. There was a small square of flecked gold near the handle, engraved to read M. Markey. Jackson tried to picture this person, based on the hard sided case, but came up empty. He wasn't good at picturing people, but as he folded his ruined trousers into the case, he pictured the young woman he had seen at the striped tent. The young woman who watched him as the sideshow fell around them.

If she hadn't swooned inside the tent, why the show for her friends? Had they been her friends at all — because those two were nowhere to be seen in the ruin. Friends, as Jackson understood, usually stayed.

Jackson slid his belt into its loops around his waist, to tighten the un-torn, but too-large trousers. He couldn't explain the three young women at all and stopped trying as the train's whistle blew. It would be dinner soon and then time to try to find sleep for a brief escape from wanting to be the other thing he was. Though he managed to hold his own cry at the sound of the whistle this time, it echoed within him. The rumble of the wheels along the track was like the flow of his blood, ceaseless and circular, running toward a horizon he could not see.

A watery horizon if the sisters were right. They said there would be water in San Francisco, but he had seen lakes before. Just big puddles, he thought, but was proved rather wrong when at last they reached the city. It was an ocean, like the Atlantic licking New York, but this Sister Mary Luke said, was the Pacific. Pacific meant calm, but Jackson didn't feel calm at the sight of it. He didn't feel anything for the water — it was the train he didn't want to leave.

He held tight to his suitcase and lingered in the doorway as others flowed toward the platform where the sisters lined them up, brushing coats into more orderly pleats. They made sure name tags were properly turned and cheeks not smudged. The sister's hand tightened briefly over his before she moved toward the platform. The train echoed empty when she went, so he dropped from the step, glancing at the train before he moved further. She bellowed steam from top and bottom, wreathing herself anew.

Priests stood on the platform and while the sisters and other children walked toward these men with eager expressions and confidence, Jackson was slower. Once accounted for, the priests and sisters shooed everyone into the depot, onto long, creaking benches. Jackson counted the panes of leaded glass in the windows while the other children were called and taken into a room. The children never emerged from the room, were only swallowed up one by one, two by two.

"Jackson."

Sister Jerome Grace stood outside the room and he forced himself to move toward her, aware of how tight his shoes pressed, how loose his coat. Everything was backwards but for the smooth, sweat-slick handle of his suitcase. It was warmer inside the small office when the door closed behind them. Jackson immediately looked for another door, breathing only when he found it on the opposite wall. Between him and the door sat a woman unlike any he had seen.

Her face looked like it had once been struck with great force, mouth and nose a little flatter than they should be. Her eyes — green like the velveteen of the train seats, like Sister Jerome Grace's eyes — were wide, perhaps from surprise carried through the years from that strike. Honey-colored hair was braided into a near beehive atop her head, laced into tight order.

Her head tilted, rouged cheek brushing the shoulder of her black fur coat. A fox's head tucked against the side of her neck, eyes glittering like violet stones. Her skirts were black, but striped with gray, and she smelled like Sunday morning breakfast at the foundling hospital, pancakes after Mass. Jackson suspected these cakes only tasted so good because they weren't allowed to eat before services.

"Hello, Jackson."

In her voice, Jackson heard a dozen low train whistles. It was that sound rumbling through him again, vibrating his bones until he expected them to shake out of his skin. He glanced down to be sure they hadn't, to be sure his wrists were covered and his hands were hands. He exhaled hard when he found it was so.

"Ma'am," he said and the sister's hand slid over his shoulder. Why had a woman like her called for a boy like him?

The woman laughed and it was the sound of falling down a rabbit hole and ending up someplace you never expected and didn't entirely understand.

"Don't need to ma'am me, but can call me Cressida. Some call me the Widow, some call me something else entirely, but you … Cressida."

Despite the wonder of Cressida, there was another in the room who commanded Jackson's attention, who had commanded it long before he looked upon any other. He looked to Sister Jerome Grace, who sat beside the priest who ensured the paperwork was in order, that Cressida actually wanted *him* of all the orphans. Why that might be, Jackson didn't care, because he realized he was to part ways with the sister.

The breath went out of him as he thought of the threads within her palm and the color of her eyes in the shade of the train car. There were three, she had said. Was Cressida one? Was this why she asked for him? He longed to ask the sister, even opened his mouth, but she shook her head — to say no, or to forestall such questions, he didn't know. Jackson swallowed the query. He clasped his hands together and tried not to leak out of his skin. He wanted so badly to fall apart, but he held to the words the sister had spoken before: he had to come to San Francisco.

Had they been in this room before? He wanted to ask the sister, but pressed tongue to teeth and held every part of himself that wanted to spill out in check.

And then they were gone — there were papers, a flurry of signatures and thank yous, and they were gone and Jackson wasn't sure who was more relived when they went, Cressida or the priests who handed him over. He and Cressida walked into the bright afternoon, into a city Jackson could not fathom, Cressida's hand on his shoulder and not the sister's. When he looked back, there was only a closed door.

Jackson wouldn't let Cressida take his suitcase. She moved toward him and he took a step away, keeping a tight grip on the handle as they walked into the city street. Cressida nodded as he dropped a few paces behind her. The fur coat she wore featured a tail spilling from her shoulder; it swayed with every step she took.

She led him to a wheeled vehicle with a metal wagon-like body lacking a hitch for a horse. He had never seen such a thing, nor had he seen the kind of man who stood nearby. Chinese often populated the penny dreadfuls he read, but Jackson had never thought to see one. The man was slight, wrapped in a loose-fitting white tunic that hid his hands and long pants falling over his feet. Gray hair was pulled into a knot at the top of his head and dark eyes narrowed on Jackson as they approached. His mouth lifted in a vague smile though, and he bowed from the waist. He said nothing, only angled his attention to Cressida, offering her a hand up to the seat.

There was not much space in the vehicle, not when the other man settled next to Cressida. Jackson clambered behind her, sitting on his suitcase as the vehicle rumbled to life.

"The people," Cressida said, "they will look as we go."

Even now people looked. As the man started the engine and set the vehicle to rumbling — not near so pleasant as the train — they looked, but it wasn't the vehicle they admired. It was Cressida. She was something from a place Jackson couldn't find a name for. With her honey hair piled tall and a fox face peeking at the world from her collar, Jackson had no idea what to make of her.

When the fur around Cressida's shoulders moved, Jackson thought it was her shifting as the vehicle pulled into the street. But Cressida stayed still. The fox face in her stole turned to pin Jackson with a violet look. Jackson stared back, skin as thin as water. The fox — if that's what it was — took a long breath, then curled back around.

They moved deeper into the city and as the scent of the ocean retreated, there came smoke and metal and something sweet. Nearly identical buildings lined long streets, gray and cinnamon stone facades with arched doorways and windows, and Jackson wondered how he would ever learn this place. The streets were tilted up and down by turns, a city on hills.

They passed over rails set into the streets and through gates of stone with tiled roofs. The vehicle wound paths Jackson had no hope to following, gliding up to one of many ordinary buildings along another straight street. Trees grew from grates in the sidewalk, golden leaves on stretching branches unable to conceal the stone letters above the building's entry. MACQUARIE'S was spelled out above an archway supported by leaf-spewing Corinthian columns. A bronze lion sat to either side of the entry, manes and claws of curled metal.

Jackson clutched his suitcase as Cressida and her man made for the doors. He followed, but stopped when the hem of his coat caught on a lion. He turned to free it only to discover the hem was clutched between the lion's teeth. Jackson stared and so did the lion, from dull bronze eyes. Patina had begun to streak its nose and paws, the former wrinkling as the teeth dug into Jackson's coat.

"Let go," Jackson said and pulled, but was rewarded with the sound of tearing wool. Jackson eased his hold, but didn't entirely let go. He glanced at Cressida and her man; they only watched. Jackson crouched, his coat large enough to allow him to get nearly nose to nose to the beast. Jackson stared, unblinking.

The lion didn't release the coat, but instead drew in a breath that sounded like wind through a drainpipe. Jackson let the lion smell him until bit by bit, the grip on his coat eased. The second lion had moved from its place at the other column, to nudge its head under Jackson's arm and take a breath of him there, too. The first lion spat Jackson's coat out — it was not wet, but warm from a broad bronze tongue. The lions moved around Jackson in tandem, knocking their heads into him, dragging their maws along his sleeves.

"They seem to approve."

Jackson watched the lions twine into Cressida's skirts, around her legs, before they withdrew and settled into their places at the base of each column.

Jackson smoothed his coat down by habit. "If they didn't?"

The tilt of Cressida's smile told him all he needed to know: if the lions hadn't approved, he wouldn't have entered the building at all. He stepped inside holding his battered suitcase as he passed through the mahogany and etched glass doors, and followed Cressida through the ordinary hall stretching out before them. The floor gleamed in a black and white checkerboard pattern, but the walls were plain, bare, and Jackson had trouble masking his disappointment. The metallic scent of the lions clung to him, but this was the only evidence anything extraordinary had happened, at least until the hall spat them into a central space that made Jackson gape.

The narrow clasp of the hall gave rise to an atrium of five floors. Stairs crisscrossed one end while a metal lift beckoned from the center of the atrium. Everything was golden wood and filigreed ironwork until the ceiling of glass panels. From this brilliant sheet, the light of the day spilled through five stories, revealing plants and trees growing up the ironwork. Something in the leaves moved, peered down, then fluttered into shadow.

"Welcome home," Cressida said, and her hand slid over his shoulder much the way Sister Jerome Grace's had.

"Y-you live here?" Jackson turned in a slow circle, to take in the stairs, the interior balconies wrapping the central space, the many doors leading to many rooms. The doors reminded him of the foundling hospital, but he had the sense there were no other children here. What possible need could she have of him?

Cressida smiled her smile again. "And so do you, little Jackson. Welcome to Macquarie's. Quiet now, but she picks up during the nighttime. Foster." She nodded to her Chinese driver who strode back to her side, hands clasped inside the loose sleeves of his tunic once more. "See that Jackson picks him a good room, then bring him down for a meal. He's nearly all bones."

Foster escorted him in the metal lift, all the way to the top floor as Jackson commanded. They rode in a comfortable silence. The Chinaman smelled like metal and Jackson wondered if it came from handling the vehicle so much.

Jackson went where he would; Foster didn't stop him from roaming. Some of the doors were locked, so Jackson presumed them already occupied, but most were open, the rooms finely ornamented and ready for whoever would stay there. It was a corner room Jackson took because from its windows and fire escape, he knew he could make it to the roof. Could climb up and watch the sky and maybe there would be pigeons.

He wasn't comfortable leaving his suitcase or taking off his coat, but he did both, telling Foster to wait in the hall while he did. Foster slipped into place beside the door as Jackson closed it, locked it, and made a slow circle in the room now his. Bed, wardrobe, nothing out of the ordinary. He supposed it was the windows that struck him most of all. They provided a view of the distant ocean and sky, and made him think of the possibility that existed outside this room. It was strange, a space he wouldn't have to share with anyone — this called to mind the hospital, the sisters, and his heart turned over at the memories, because he came back to the Chicago sideshow, to the taste of that man against his teeth. He came back to the sister's hand opening under her scissors and he wanted to be cut open. To see what was inside.

Jackson was mindful of the room's condition and feeling like a trespasser, he hung his coat on the provided rack and slipped his suitcase under the bed, hiding it with a flip of the bedspread. He didn't allow himself time to become any more used to the room. He had no key for the door until Foster produced a ring of them and found the proper one for the lock. It was iron, black enough to smudge a person's hand. Foster offered it up without a word after locking the door. Jackson slipped it into his pocket and the entire way to find food, his hand curled around it, tight. It became immediately his.

Foster took him through the lower level of the building, through corridors opening into countless secret spaces. It was a city all its own, wood paneled walls and richly carpeted floors, and by the time they reached Cressida, Jackson could not say how many twists and turns they had taken. It was a maze of unfathomed delights. As golden as the outer rooms had been, the room Foster took him to was dark, the wood having been polished so well Jackson could see his own watery reflection in the panels as he crossed to Cressida's table.

Gold and crimson fabric spilled from the ceiling, clouds of billowing ivory suspended from chandeliers of spun sugar. The chandeliers held hundreds upon hundreds of candles, the uprush of heat keeping the ceiling in constant motion. Ivory linen and silver spread across Cressida's table, a small mountain of pearlescent candles in its center spilling more golden light.

"Come."

Cressida patted the bench beside her. She had removed her stole to reveal the simple black of the dress she wore, the color of mourning even if the skirts were striped with gray. Jackson sat, but his gaze didn't settle. He took in the long bar of glass and gold across the room, a mirror set along its backside to reflect the entire room. An equally long stage for performers twined amid the tables. It wasn't straight, but wove its way like a snake through the room. Its wood was a shade darker than the walls and floor, giving the impression of shadow, whereas the bar shone like the sun under all the candles.

"You're of an age I won't keep you from any place in Macquarie's," Cressida said. She reached for a bottle and poured the dark and bubbling contents into the glass before him. It looked like soda water, but was dark as pitch, and when Jackson sipped, it was surprisingly sweet. "But you won't drink while working, and you won't touch the ladies."

Jackson set his glass down. "Ladies, ma'am?"

As if they had been prompted by his words, the draped fabric at the far end of the stage fluttered and parted, allowing a trio of young women into the room. They didn't look at Cressida or Jackson, only set to going through the motions of their performance. They were dressed in nearly nothing, what little they wore held on by breath alone, gleaming silver strings and trails of translucent fabric concealing a curve of flesh only to reveal it again each time they moved. Far worse than these glimpses of flesh was the flesh itself. It was translucent like the fabric, exposing shadows of corded muscles beneath the skin. Up the line of a spine, he could almost see bones; the women looked strangely manufactured, skin pulling taut over shelled rib cages as one body bowed into another.

Jackson fought to find a proper breath. "Work, ma'am?"

Plates heaped with food appeared at the table, brought by men and women who looked like Foster with their loose tunics and narrowed eyes. Jackson recognized only one meal on the table, roasted rabbit dredged in flour and butter so it would crisp. His mouth watered and Cressida nodded, silently telling him not to wait. Other plates were added, some manner of bird in jelly, pickled beets, parsnips fried in molasses. Jackson served himself, filling up the empty plate Foster offered him. He held his fork like a shovel, molasses coating his tongue in a tarry slick as he poked the parsnips down.

"I wanted to give you a home, little Jackson, but everyone works for what they have." Cressida's eyes drifted to the three young women who moved silently on the stage. "Everyone has a part to play. I heard of your unique gifts from the sisters and knew you would come here and be part of this family."

Jackson coughed, a wedge of rabbit lodged in his throat. "G-gifts, ma' —"

"Don't you goddamn ma'am me again," she said gently, though her eyes betrayed her anger in the way they snapped from the girls and landed on him. "You will not be coy in this place. You have hidden yourself away, I know — it's the way of your kind in this world, when you find yourself in a place you don't fit, a place that don't rightly hold you, but here ..." She spread her hands to encompass more than the room. Jackson thought she meant the entire city. "That doesn't have to be the case. You are yourself here, only that. None shall harm you."

The women slipped in and out of the drapes, showing a brief length of translucent leg before allowing the fabric to swallow it back up. Jackson's grip tightened on his fork and it exploded from his grasp, skewering the mountain of candles in the center of the table. His hand was no longer a hand, but an abrupt mass of writhing coils. He swallowed hard and flushed, but Cressida looked at him with pride alone.

The first problem with leaving his room via the window was the girl on the fire escape.

Jackson stared at her through the pane of glass, his hand poised on the latch. His meal settled into his stomach in a hard lump and his mouth grew dry, like he hadn't consumed all of the sweet soda Cressida kept pouring. His arms shook with fine tremors — he wasn't cold or fearful at the sight of the girl, only confused.

When at last he convinced his normal fingers to turn the latch, he pulled the window open, to stare at the girl who had stared at him outside the wreck of the Chicago sideshow.

She was maybe his age and the meeting held a strange clarity, one he would think on for years to come. She appeared drawn in sharply inked lines; he could see everything there was to see as if noonday sun shone down, but it was dark, the sky moonless but for her own pale and rounded face. Although the girl wore trousers now — outrageous! — and her hair was drawn into a severe knot at the nape of her neck, Jackson knew he wouldn't forget those black eyes.

"Five stories up," he said. Had she pulled the fire escape ladder down and climbed up? It was the most reasonable thought, but then again, there was a girl. On his fire escape. What was reasonable?

Dust coated her trousers and her hands rested filthy on the metal. She didn't wear a jacket despite the cool air of the night, only what looked like a man's shirt, buttoned up to her neck. The buttons glowed and wavered, like pearls under water. Jackson dashed a hand over his eyes and she came back into solid focus. She said nothing.

The tremors in his arms moved through his chest, into hips and legs, and he couldn't stand still. Jackson pulled the other side of the window open and hoisted himself onto the fire escape. The girl sat up, but did not say a word. Jackson smiled at her, the structure of his mouth slipping to reveal more tooth than a person rightly should. This close, she smelled like the sweat of climbing over roofs and deeper down, almond soap. Not at all the flowers and pixies he imagined. She smelled like leather too and when at last she drew herself to a height even with him, he saw the coil of leather at her waist. A whip.

"You ain't no regular girl," he said, and then nodded up, to the starry sky above. "C'mon."

He heard her climbing the ladder after him, boots on rung after rung until they stood side by side on the roof. She wasn't even breathing hard and while Jackson was, he didn't care. Up here, everything was clear, like the skins of Macquarie's dancers. She walked past him, like she'd been up here a dozen times before, confident and true, so Jackson followed and eventually bypassed her, to stare through the glass and iron panels making up the sunroof. He could see down into the bottom of the building.

"You ain't no regular boy. The Widow adopt you?"

It wasn't the voice he expected her to have. Just like she didn't smell like flowers or fancy, she didn't sound like a lady and he liked that about her. He straightened to watch her prowl around him. She looked at him and not the roof, eyes constantly assessing. He had no coat, nor certainly any weapon, only the strange assuredness that shot through him the way the dark drink had. His chin came up and if he'd had fur, it might have bristled.

"What of it? What do you know of Cressida anyhow?"

Her mouth split in a smile, the first expression he'd seen of her other than intent study. She stopped pacing, hands resting on her hips. There was no moon, but Jackson would have sworn (and would swear years later) there was, because there was a light in the girl's eyes, milky and liquid, a thing he could drink down and not regret.

"You want to be careful in a place like this," she said. Her left hand fingered her whip. "A woman like the Widow ain't no normal woman, if you take my meaning." Her eyes narrowed, a slight fluctuation to the light in her eyes. "No reason she'd want a normal boy ..."

Her voice trailed off and she closed the distance between them. Jackson thought she was going to kiss him — he could almost taste her mouth and not having been kissed, he could only imagine the things it might taste like. Flowers were right out, he decided. Maybe she tasted like bubbling soda, like the brown almond cookie he'd had after. Crisp and sweet.

She didn't kiss him. Her hand closed on his chin, dirty fingers pressing into his skin. Her lips parted but there was no kiss, no word, only a soft breath. When she exhaled, it was hard and through her nose. Jackson had once seen a group of card players; she reminded him of them, a man vexed with the choices before him.

"This city is both big and small," she said, keeping hold of him. "You don't have to go far to find entertainments more pleasing than Macquarie's."

If she been a dancer, she might have swayed her hips to tempt him even more than she already had by simply *being*. She stood stock still, hand clenching his cheek, fingers on her whip. His body shifted, began to bleed into what he wanted to be. He pulled himself back from that edge.

"Bell's is two blocks north, other side of the street from the bakery."

With that, she released him. She took a step back and Jackson sucked in a breath. She smelled like sweat and soap, even as she walked away. She walked backwards, keeping her eyes on him all the while. As if she had walked this roof a dozen times. Had they been on this roof before? Jackson could not remember, did not want to remember, because on its own this moment was sweet and he thought he was flying. The sky was clear and cold and he could feel her hand wrapped in his own. He did not move after her, for fear she would evaporate.

"My name is Jackson," he said before she got too far away.

She didn't offer her name, only turned from him and ran. She didn't evaporate, but moved so quickly to the far edge of the building she might as well have. Jackson's eyes widened — time slowed, she was going to run out of building, she was going to —

She slipped over the edge and was gone. As if a hot iron had been placed against his backside, he ran. The other edge of the building had a fire escape too — his heart lodged in his throat as he leaned there, hands having dissolved to coils whipping against the roof edge. But the fire escape stood empty. There was no sign of her there, nor was she shattered in the street. She was simply gone.

Life at Macquarie's settled into a routine. Cressida often dispatched him with Foster, but from there, Jackson could have no expectations.

Each day was never like another. As much as he enjoyed the environment, he ached to leave it, if only to go north and discover Bell's and the black-eyed girl. Their path of errands never took them north and he asked Foster why that was, as they left Macquarie's to restock staples for the pantry.

Foster hesitated. Jackson had no doubt the man worked within a certain set of guidelines — much as Cressida had told him not to touch the ladies or drink while working. Foster had been here for five years. He wouldn't say where his family had gone, but Jackson suspected they had been deported, along with countless other Chinese.

"Northways is not our territory," Foster said, hoisting a sack of flour over his shoulder as they made to leave the store. His voice was nearly melodic, but it dropped lower now. The storekeeper gave them a nod as they left — everyone was always exceedingly cordial when they came for supplies. Jackson knew Cressida was a woman of wealth and means, but didn't know how she had come to be such.

"Not our territory." Jackson contemplated that, as they placed the sacks in the back of the automobile. "Does that mean we can't go there? Ever?" He found the idea of territories immediately familiar, a leftover from the foundling hospital. It was reasonable for the kids to establish their boundaries in such a way, obliterating anyone who dared venture inside lines they had not drawn.

"Business might take us there." Foster slid into the driver's seat and waited for Jackson to sit. "But it typically will not. A person should have all they need inside their own space, isn't it so? Everything we need truly exists within the walls of Macquarie's and Cressida gives us all we require. Our needs do not expand northways."

Jackson's needs, however, did expand northways. He thought of north when he went to sleep. He thought of north when he got up each morning. He spent evenings on the roof, wondering if he could make it there by rooftops alone, so none might know, and when he found the metal cat-walk connecting Macquarie's to another building, he rejoiced. Every day worked him to exhaustion, but he ventured to the roof every night, daring to cross the catwalk high above the streets below. The roof of the building led to another and this to another, and he traced his way to the building opposite what must be Bell's, but could not reach Bell's itself. Not this way.

He took to sitting on the catwalk in most of his natural form. He could take his shoes off and let his feet fall into the coils they wanted to be. He reminded himself to roll his trousers to his thighs and control the change so he wasn't constantly ruining what few clothes he had. Cressida would have understood; she had told him to be what he was without shame or doubt, but he always remembered the foundling hospital and the constant lack of everything. His circumstances had changed, but he treasured all he had been given, not throwing it carelessly away simply because he could.

He watched as customers left Bell's in the small hours of morning, would smell the change in the air as warm bodies left close spaces. They smelled of smoke, liquor, and perfume. Of sweat and things Jackson could not put a name to. They left singly, and in pairs, and sometimes in trios. He watched as the windows of upstairs rooms brightened with gas- and candlelight, figures twining together, then parting.

He wondered which room was hers. If she brought anyone back with her, if it was part of her job or simply a pleasure she took. He wondered if she could see him, if she watched Macquarie's the way he watched Bell's.

Only once did he see her, one early morning on the street that would lead her to Macquarie's. Was she looking for him? The idea was absurd, but it made him smile. It wasn't Macquarie's she went to, vanishing in-stead into Kotler's Bakery. She emerged later with a neatly tied package that revealed itself to be palmiers when she untied the blue ribbon. The pastries vanished one by one into her mouth and he thought *oh to be so sweet, that she might swallow me, that I might dissolve upon her tongue.*

One block south of Macquarie's, Chinatown sprawled. He followed Foster into the teeming streets and focused on not staring too long at any one thing, for fear he would miss the next captivating person or place. He chafed at not being allowed to go far on his own, but was thankful for Foster the deeper they roamed. Cressida didn't formally claim these streets — Foster said she couldn't, if she wanted to stay on good terms with the Chinese — however good portions of them were under her dominion and protection even so.

Inventory from small shops spilled out onto the sidewalks in baskets, on tables and rugs, lining wood shelves. Any food Jackson could imagine and most he could not were easily found, from roasted ducks gleaming in windows, to neatly arrayed steamed buns filled with sweets or savories. They stopped at one vendor to collect a payment and the man included a paper sack filled with fried merelings. Jackson took them for squid or shrimp, which they were often hauled in with, until he tasted them and found them saltier beneath the fried breading. Mermaid tails, Foster told him, were a delicacy anywhere. Jackson crunched through another and could see why.

The building they headed toward was a compact three stories. Most of the buildings in Chinatown were smaller, Jackson saw, unless the building was a pagoda. Foster explained how important this building was, noting its glossy lacquered doors, blue columns, and seafoam green roof tiles. Everything about the building spoke to its importance amid the darker storefronts that filled the rest of the street. Iron lions crouched beside the entry, but they knew Foster, and bowed their heads, allowing them entry.

It was a simple transaction inside a room smelling of salt water, its walls lined with gurgling tanks. The tanks held creatures Jackson wanted to inventory: octopus and fish with rainbow scales, live merelings, infant krakens. The merelings were bigger than those Jackson had just eaten, enough older that they were aware of the world outside their tank; their small hands pressed to the glass and they watched.

The leader of the tong, the honorable Lee Jun-fan, bowed before Foster and offered a slim envelope crafted from brocaded silks of gold and blue. Foster did not open it, but plainly knew by the weight he had been given the correct payment. There was only relief in Lee's eyes when Foster smiled and offered a bow in return. Jackson watched, understanding this man was indebted to Cressida and her people.

"The Widow sends her regards to your honorable family," Foster said, "and assures you the pestilence of recent weeks will have passed into the west, as does the setting sun each evening. The ocean swallows such filth and it is never seen to rise again."

Lee bowed again. When he crossed his arms over his chest, his hands curled into his tunic. "The Widow is truly kind in her provisions. Does she require ..."

One hand unknotted to gesture to a tank with a kraken inside. The beast looked made of stone until it moved. One looping tentacle curled up and out of the water, to delve into the neighboring tank where it scooped out a mereling. The mereling shrieked, its violet and green scaled tail flicking water as it thrashed in panic. The mereling went silent, pulled under the waters of the kraken's tank, then vanished in a poof of blood.

"Not at this time," Foster said with a slight shake of his head. "Of course, should she require such, one of us will return."

Foster didn't introduce him to Lee, and Jackson didn't question it. Lee seemed about to quake out of his shoes. Jackson had little doubt he would be remembered by the man if Cressida or Foster sent him alone here. When they left the building, Foster opened the brocade pouch to pour golden fish and skulls into his palm. Foster didn't count what he had been given, only handed Jackson the empty pouch and began to eat the gold. He didn't chew, just set each piece on his tongue and swallowed.

"Pretty neat trick."

The voice came from across the street. Jackson's attention snapped that way, taking in the four young men who approached. Other pedestrian traffic in the street peeled back as they crossed the road. They were young and though white, looked to spend their days consumed by hard work. Their hands were rough, their shoulders broad, as if they lifted shipping containers at the docks from sunup to sundown.

"Samuel," Foster said and bowed at the waist, as if greeting a friend.

Another of the young men spoke, a condescending laugh edging his words. Jackson recognized the tone from his time in the foundling hospital. "Too bad he can't shit them back out — either way, getting it back won't be pretty."

"Duncan," Foster said and Jackson watched him bow again. Calm, welcoming.

Jackson didn't know what they meant by shitting the gold out, but the lack of pretty made itself apparent when the boys lunged, fists flying. Maybe they meant to rip the money out of Foster; Jackson wasn't going to wait to find out.

Instinct took over and it didn't matter how old these men were, how big, or where they were in the city. Jackson let the transformation come. He thought sure the Chinese had seen stranger and if he meant to eat these young men, it didn't matter what they saw. His gaping maw and then the blackness. That was all there would be.

He had seen plenty of brawls, but his fights in the foundling hospital had chiefly been one on one. Once the kids discovered the strength behind small fists that were no longer small fists but slapping coils, they didn't approach. This, two on four, was a strange concept, made easier when Foster moved to divide the four into two, so they each might take a pair. Samuel and Duncan moved for Jackson, leaving Foster the other two.

But Foster, Jackson saw, was not entirely Foster; he too had changed, human form shifting to something Other. Gone was his tidy topknot, gray hair having swallowed his head and shoulders. Foster was a fierce thing, looking part dragon, part dog, the knot of hair having become a single sharpened antler Foster slashed toward the two men nearest him.

The admiration Jackson knew was strange. In the foundling hospital, no one had stood beside him. When conflict came, most ran if they weren't the instigators. Fighting *with* someone as opposed to against them was something Jackson could hardly comprehend.

When his fist hit Samuel, it was only a fist, slamming into cheek and jaw. But Jackson quickly dissolved fingers into coils, lashing them around Samuel's throat to keep him from toppling to the ground. Held at a slight distance, Samuel couldn't even gather breath to scream.

Wading into the fight, Duncan drew a pair of knives from his belt. Jackson would have thought him more timid, but he didn't hesitate. Hesitation was death; the orphan in Jackson knew it the way he knew breathing, the way he knew the bite of the blades as Duncan slashed out with both. Jackson's hold on Samuel tightened, but his choked breath didn't deter Duncan.

Blades whirled and gleamed in the gaslights like a dozen angry snakes. Disregarding them, Jackson lunged forward, using Samuel as a shield, hoisting him into Duncan. The knives flashed down, away, the weakness Jackson sought. Jackson pressed the advantage, snapping one leg coil around Duncan's legs. From the back, Jackson pulled and sent him sprawling to the street. With Duncan down, Jackson thrust Samuel into the blades.

Samuel sucked in a gurgled breath as he went down, but the damage was done. Fresh blood welled through Samuel's shirt and Jackson was only satisfied to see it, evidence of his job well done. He could nearly taste the blood in the air and dipped his head closer.

"You know the price for coming into these streets," Foster snarled to the quartet through his fanged mouth. The two men he had fought staggered back, slashed and bleeding as Duncan tried to pick Samuel up. Jackson stared at the blade in Samuel's side, at the sudden pale cast to his skin. Samuel would be cold soon and wouldn't care.

Duncan spat blood in Foster's direction. "You tell the Widow —"

"Nothing." Foster shook his head, calm as a lake in the middle of winter. With the head shake, some semblance of humanity returned to him. The antler melted away, fur retreating as skin came to the fore. But that skin was streaked with blue blood carrying a strange, oily tang. "You are beneath the Widow's worries. You have no place in this city. Like the rats, you simply don't know it yet. You will sink into the sewers and be swallowed by the floods."

Jackson drew himself into his normal skin, but it was difficult with blood everywhere. He wanted to swallow all four of the men and when Foster let them hobble off, Jackson spat and snarled.

"You *let* them go?"

Foster turned, humanity restored, the sealing of a mask back into place. "Samuel, James, Duncan, and Theo," he said, calmly scraping his sweat-slick hair back from his face. He coiled his hair back into a knot, dark eyes surveying Jackson all the while. "The Bell brothers."

Bell's is two blocks north, she had said. Two blocks north ... where their business did not extend. Jackson clenched his teeth, matters becoming more clear to him.

"The Widow wants them dead, make no mistake," Foster continued.

He nodded up the street the way they had come and Jackson fell into step beside him. People were beginning to reemerge from their homes and businesses. "But not like this."

"Then how?" Jackson glanced back at the blood splattered in the street. Already merchants were bringing buckets of water to wash it away, as though it had never been.

Foster's mouth moved into the shadow of a smile. "In careful ways, young Jackson. Their father is wrathful, like you have not seen, and he would move against her should she give him an opening. He would have her territory, he would have her ..." Foster's thin shoulders moved slightly beneath his tunic. "Everything."

Back inside Macquarie's, Foster bent to the floor, doubled over as if in pain. But there was only joy as he spat the golden skulls and fish onto the rug. Jackson slid a hand over the man's shoulder, wishing to comfort him if he might, but Foster shook his head and kneeled there, smiling darkly. The scent of hot metal rose thick around them.

Later, Jackson supposed he might understand, how holding a thing for a while could give a person pleasure; while later spitting it out could do the same. It was much the same way with him and his forms. Some days, there was pleasure in denying what he was. As he undressed in the low lights of his room, he also came to understand exactly what those boys tonight had been about. They hadn't wanted to kill anyone. They wanted to know what they were up against with the new kid.

Jackson supposed that now, they knew.

North of Macquarie's, the city block ran straight, up a hill and over, but before one went over, there sat Bell's, a building as impressive as Macquarie's, if wholly different. Where Macquarie's was the color of broken earth, Bell's was the color of a clouded sky, white streaked with gray. This sky had never known blue, only clouds. Every window and corner was marked with wrought iron, the metal carrying into the lettering above the doors, between gas lamps spilling amber light everywhere.

Two ivory gargoyles framed the main door, the people streaming into the venue passing under the arching wings. Jackson wondered if these people knew the gargoyles were alive; he watched their eyes as the beasts watched the crowd, counting every person who went in, assuring each paid their entry fee. A boy younger than Jackson tried to slip past, huddled in the shadow of an older man.

The gargoyle on left made the move, snatching the child from the mass of patrons, causing the others to draw back with shrieks. Jackson was captivated by the way the gargoyle lifted the kid toward its mouth. Surely the gargoyle didn't mean to —

The kid vanished into the gargoyle's stony maw, his terrified shriek cut off midway through. Jackson expected blood, expected something, but all was silence until the crowd milled forward again, making their payments unquestionably visible to the creatures. The gargoyle tucked itself back into place and Jackson envisioned the kid, in the black of the beast's belly. What else was in there?

Cressida paid him a reasonable wage, and saw too he had spending money. She didn't mind him exploring the city — wanted him to learn its ways — but he didn't tell her he was going to Bell's. Based on what the girl had said to him, he worried there was something more at play here.

He paid his coin to get in and expected some hassle; expected the hawker at the door to tell him he was too young, he was too poor, he was too something, but they ushered him in alongside the others.

"Think she'll be here?"

"Of course she'll be here."

Jackson's thoughts went straight to the girl from the roof. His throat tightened at the idea she would be like the dancers Cressida employed. Translucent and spread for all to see. Something inside him rebelled at this idea. She wasn't like those dancers, a thing for men to —

His mind wouldn't go there (though of course it already had, and slowly, over the curve of her cheek and mouth, thinking back to that longed-for kiss). She could very well be here for that reason. Women in the city were scarce. It was one reason Macquarie's packed in crowds every night. Hardworking men needed their diversions after long days, didn't they? Warm spaces, inhabited by women who took on the guise of living works of art; women more liquid in their motions than solid, bending as one would bend them. Curls of cigar smoke, deep snifters of brandy, and shadows deep enough between the candlelit spaces that one didn't care what another did.

Bell's was nothing like Macquarie's. A foyer led to three sets of double doors, and these opened into a vast theater with rows of seats on a balcony level, and clustered tables on the lower level. While men streamed up curving staircases toward the balcony, Jackson threaded his way through the crowd, wanting to be as close as possible to the half-moon stage filling an entire far wall.

White velvet curtains poured from the ceiling, pooling on the polished cherrywood stage, globes of gaslights tracing a ring around the stage's outer edge. Above the stage, a myriad of cords and cables dangled, while a small orchestra occupied a pit in the floor just beyond the stage's outer edge. Jackson wondered if performers would fly on the cables, but amid the jostling for position, and the music, he didn't ask. The curtains parted and the crowd erupted.

Jackson counted each woman as they came onto the stage, each more lavishly costumed than the last. They flowed like water from some hidden stream, in twos and then threes. Jackson saw no muscle or bone through their skins, only the gleam of gaslight on exposed legs, breasts, and arms. Chiffon and crinoline wrapped them, silks and laces and brocades, and Jackson knew without a doubt he had never seen anything so extraordinary.

Sixteen women in total were made to look like carousel animals. While there were a couple horses, one cream and one black, there was also a zebra, a giraffe, an elephant, and a splendid whale. Jackson wondered how the women kept from stepping on its trailing tail, then watched in wonder as the tail rose behind the woman's back, her skirts also lifting. The uprush of fabric resembled a furious blue-white wave. Jackson stared.

He also looked for her, the black-eyed girl from the roof, but he did not see her and tried to contain his disappointment. If Bell's was anything like Macquarie's, there was more to come and these were not all the entertainers. Jackson sucked in a breath that smelled of smoke and men, and let the wonder of the gaslight on skin and sequin carry him to another place.

The whale danced off, giving way for beasts Jackson could not name. Glittering wings and writhing coils rioted in tandem as this living carousel rotated across the stage. A snake bowed into the black horse, slithering over the belly and around, until the women were kissing, black lips notched to white. Jackson's body came alive in ways he wished it would not.

The entire audience erupted in applause but Jackson remained silent. Silent and aware he was holding tightly to his human form. He wanted to bleed into the thing he truly was, but he thought of those gargoyles and of being swallowed. He thought of missing the black-eyed girl should she appear and so he held fast.

He was unprepared when she did appear. The carousel girls fanned around the edge of the stage, chests heaving from their exertions, and another set of curtains parted. These gave way to the black-eyed girl, who strode down the center of the stage in a dress very like the one she had worn in Chicago. Plain, simple, white, and buttoned to the neck. The gaslights burnished her brown curls, hands covered by prim white gloves.

The music swelled, then went silent. The hall held its breath and Jackson could not move as the lights dimmed. The black-eyed girl hovered between this place and that, a shadow he lost sight of. Then, the lights returned, exploding into full brightness. Jackson lost his vision for a breath, as if he had looked at the sun and could see only shadows, after images of actual people. If one had looked away from the girl, it might seem the explosion of light had burned her dress clean off. Jackson was only learning the ways of showmanship, but was so focused on her, he could not miss the snap of her wrist to part what few laces held her dress and gloves together. The discarded fabric vanished into a slim vent in the stage floor.

Black leather covered her from head to toe, trousers clinging to her round bottom and legs, a corset pinching her in tight at the waist before swelling across breasts. Her shoulders were bare, so pale they might have been carved from alabaster and those in the audience who didn't applaud, made a low murmur. It was lecherous to Jackson's ears and he hated them all. Hated what they surely thought when they saw her, for he thought it too.

At her waist, she wore her whip and she drew it loose, allowing it to slither to the floor. Her hands were protected by leather gloves, but Jackson was aware of every finger, how they held the hard whip handle, how they moved as she spun the whip. He was aware too of the way her entire body shifted in reaction to the new beasts on the stage.

The carousel girls held their positions, a beautiful cage for the five lions spilling from another set of curtains. Part of the audience recoiled, but most fell into shocked silence, as the orchestra hummed and the black-eyed girl lifted her whip. She never struck the animals, only told them where to go with the whip's hiss and pop. The lions circled her in a run, then leapt onto the cages and platforms wheeled into place by the zebra and hippo of the carousel. Jackson knew of lions from the zoo and from books, and those guarding the doors throughout the city, but to see these here, under her command, took every breath from him.

Jackson moved from the edge of the stage and slid into an empty chair, watching with his hands tented in front of his face. Pieces of him slipped away; his mind wandered down avenues he could not explain or understand. He pictured this girl as a woman and he knew her name for it was soft in his mouth even as he bit into the flesh of her bottom lip, inside a moving train, bundled into his very own bed. He knew the scent of her beyond the soap the rest of the world knew. He knew the color of the shadow tracing the length of her bare thigh. He was sickened by it and lifted up in the same instant.

Have we been here before? He had asked the sister and he wanted to ask this girl. Was she the third in this trio of women? Was Cressida? Jackson's head ached and he shifted in the chair, into the sudden swell of a body beside his. The carousel women had slipped down from the stage, to roam amid the crowd, and the whale smiled at him. Up close, her eyelashes and eyebrows were decorated with blue stones and a dust sparkling under the gaslights like stars. Her lips were painted into a full blue pout. White sea froth curled down her neck, into her bosom, while her white hair was piled three hand-spans high, the whale tail rising up behind it.

"Haven't seen you here before, little one."

Jackson stared, unable to do anything else. He was aware of the black-eyed girl on stage, of the lions as they continued to shift under the direction of her whip, but this woman before him was something altogether different. She leaned in, bringing Jackson's hand against her shoulder.

Her skin was unbearably warm and soft.

"Newcomers are entitled to a free swim ... you do know how to swim?" She leaned in so close Jackson could see the sheen of sweat dotting her upper lip. Could see too the shadow of a beard that clung there. Jackson dared touch her then, his hand careful along the line of her jaw, tipping her head up just a little, to study the neck, to take in the Adam's apple, curiously male amid the froth of femininity.

Jackson leaned back, his hand gentle on the whale's chin. "You're a man." There was a question in his voice, his mind trying to catch up to what his eyes had seen.

The painted blue mouth curled up in a slow smile. "Suppose you came for Mae then." He nodded toward the stage, to the girl and her lions. "They mostly do, but there are others ..."

One of these others came up behind the beautiful whale, hands sliding up the tail rising in an arc over the piled white hair before circling around to cup the breasts that could not be breasts at all. This man nuzzled the whale's cheek and the whale grinned, leaning back into his eager body.

"There are others," Jackson repeated, and watched as the pair slid off into the shadows clogging the outskirts of the theater floor. He thought the world would somehow fall out from under him, that nothing would make a lick of sense, but the more he looked, the more things *did* make sense. Everything was a lie and everything remained beautiful. Maybe it was beautiful *because* it was a lie.

He brought his attention back to the girl on the stage, Mae. He whispered her name, letting it be lost to the crowd adoring her, that marveled at her and her lions, but it was mostly her they adored. He no longer reviled them, but understood. They came for the show, for the artifice, for the beautiful lie spread in the gaslight before them. They could have that. Jackson wanted more.

A paper lion fluttered from the railing of Jackson's fire escape, tied with a white ribbon that could have come from Mae's white dress. He slid onto the metal balcony and untied the beacon, looking up the ladder to the roof. At its apex, another lion twisted in the night air. He untied the first lion, cut from heavy paper and colored with pen and pencil. A red painted ribbon decorated its neck.

Jackson slid the paper lion between his teeth and climbed. He lingered at the edge of the roof, looking for her before he hauled himself up. Mae stood at the furthest edge, near the first catwalk. Jackson tugged the second lion free and held both as he crossed to her. She was dressed in trousers again, a trim jacket, her hair twisted under the collar. If someone didn't know her, they might take her for a boy.

He drew within a step of her before she turned, before her balled fist closed the distance slammed into his jaw. Unprepared, he went down. The paper lions fluttered to the roof, forgotten as he tried to understand, but she didn't give him time. The next thing he knew was the wrap of her whip around his throat.

"Theo will live, no thanks to you."

Jackson tried to reply, but she pulled tight on the whip making speech an uncomfortable thing at best. He sucked in a breath instead, both hands spread wide. "M —"

Mae coiled the whip into her hand, shortening the length of leather between them as she crouched down. Jackson had never seen eyes so angry.

"I'm not going to kill you because you didn't kill them," she continued with a sharp pull on the whip. His back angled up from the roof so he might not lose his entire ability to breathe. "Because I know how these things go. They just wanted to know what you were, newcomer." Her upper lip curled in a sneer. "Snake."

The whip unspooled from his neck with a snake-like hiss of its own. Jackson flopped back hard, staring at the distant stars as Mae moved off. He thought he could see galaxies moving in the dark, but was only aware of the sound of her, of her whip as she coiled it to her belt and exhaled. Jackson rolled to his shoulder, plucked the paper lions from the roof, and stood.

"Right," Jackson said. His hand went to his throat, to touch the warm line her whip had left behind. Had the leather burned him? He somehow thought not; her hand was steady and sure. He stared at Mae's back, the taut way she held herself, and he thought of the young man he'd thrust into the knives, of the other three with him. "What is Theo to you, then? He works for Bell's like you?"

"He is a Bell." She looked at him over his shoulder as he drew even with her, then looked northward to Bell's again. "My brothers."

What little warmth the evening air contained drained away. Mae had come to his roof to find out what he was and, having been disappointed, her brothers trailed after, getting a firmer answer to their questions. It didn't stop his hands from shaking.

"You came?" She had turned around, attention fully on him now. Her arms were crossed over her jacket, hands tucked into armpits like she was cold. "To see the show?"

Jackson lifted the paper lions. "*Your* show." The white ribbons lifted in the night breeze and he remembered the way her dress vanished on stage. Remembered the queer feeling in his belly. "You know I did."

Mae's jaw tightened and she reached for the lions, but Jackson held them out of her reach, his arm extended above his head. He was transported back to the shadowed hospital halls, other boys holding his penny dreadfuls out of reach, demanding money for them.

Mae didn't step away, but drew her hand back, tucking it under her arm again. Her cheeks were pinker than they had been. "Did you enjoy it?"

She smelled warm in the cool night, like leather and lemon, and Jackson kept his face carefully neutral. If she was a Bell, she was dangerous, but then, she had been dangerous before he knew her affiliations. Dangerous sitting on the edge of his fire escape. Dangerous with those lions under her command. He took a step back and tucked the paper lions into his own pocket. "You know I did."

The silence between them ran like a ribbon, smooth and not uncomfortable. Jackson kept his hands in his pockets, feeling the lions someone had colored, stroking a ribbon between thumb and forefinger as he watched her watch the city.

"They seem human," he eventually said. When she looked over, that silent knowing in her eyes, he added, "Your brothers." He watched as the muscle in her jaw tensed again, the only outward sign of her annoyance.

"Strange, that," she said, and let her hands drop from their tucked position. "Come with me." She turned, her boots not making a sound on the roof as she moved off.

Jackson stared after her, but not for long. He took double steps to fall into step beside her as she crossed the roof. He was rewarded with a smug smile from her, one that made him bristle, but as she crossed the catwalk and led him across the neighboring building, he didn't care. She could be as smug as she wanted. She knew this city and he didn't. He would follow her lead for now, because it *would* lead him somewhere. Besides, he had stabbed her brother and she had come calling even so. Surely that meant something.

Nothing.

Everything.

Have we been here before?

He told the sister's whispering voice to shut it and stayed close behind Mae when she slipped one level down a fire escape. This escape led to another catwalk and they crossed in silence, unknown to everyone on the street below. There was power up here, in knowing these routes when those below did not.

Counting the buildings as they went became something of an obsession, an invisible trail of breadcrumbs in his mind. Mae never hesitated, not even to see if he was keeping up. Where she went, he followed, up iron ladders, across narrow catwalks.

The building she led him to was across from the docks, the scent of the ocean washing up to greet them. They crouched in a shadow falling over a fire escape, behind someone's forgotten laundry. Mae peered over the rail, then pointed to one ship in particular. Cressida's vehicle trundled into the scene.

Jackson's hands curled around the fire escape grate as Foster parked the automobile. Cressida poured out in her black skirts and fox wrap. The fox surveyed the street behind her. She and Foster moved toward the ship and the men who emerged from it.

"What is this?" Jackson asked, looking again to Mae.

"This is a problem," Mae said, "but I don't expect you to see it that way yet. The Widow controls so much of this city and she … Just watch."

Cressida accepted a sheaf of papers from one of the men and carefully read through them. She questioned one thing, her gloved finger stroking over a line, but the captain nodded and gestured into the darkness between the berthed ships. Cressida stepped into the dark and the captain followed. Jackson shifted, trying to get a better look, but Mae's hand forestalled him from actually leaving the fire escape to get closer.

"Just wait."

It was an eternity, wondering where Cressida had gone and what had come in on the ship. When the riddle was at last solved, Jackson wasn't sure what to think. Cressida and the captain emerged from the darkness and it was just them walking and talking, papers held in Cressida's hand. Then, other figures began to emerge.

These human-like shapes peeled away from clotted darkness; Jackson was certain if he was close enough, he would have heard a wet puckering kiss as they separated from the black. A chill having nothing to do with the cool evening slid down his spine.

"What the hell are *those*?"

Mae shook her head. "We don't know." Her voice had dropped to a whisper, but she didn't look away. Jackson counted the shadowy forms as they emerged. Four, six, eight, twelve. They kept coming.

A metal trunk perched in the back of the automobile and Foster opened it, allowing the shadowed forms to slide inside. The way steam might escape a teapot, these creatures were swallowed by the metal, locked inside when Foster closed the lid.

"What do you mean you don't know what they are?" Jackson lowered his voice, but it held a panicked edge. "You're supposed to know what they are. You have issues with the Wid — With Cressida. You bring me here. To see this." He jabbed a hand toward the automobile. "You are supposed to know —"

Mae's hand around his throat silenced him. "If I knew what those things were, do you think I would be playing this game? *You* might have known. This is the third … shipment at least. There may have been others we didn't see, but this … The third. There have been at least twenty of those things in each run. They always go into that metal box. She's …" Mae shook her head, and Jackson thought she was trying to find the right words, but a look in her eyes told him otherwise. She was holding back tears and it made something inside him come loose.

His hand covered hers, to pull hers away from his throat so he might talk. But he wasn't sure what to say then, either. They sat there, as Cressida went on her way. The ship's captain vanished amid the ships and — Jackson still held Mae's hand. He abruptly dropped it, her black stare nailing him where he sat.

"She's planning something," Mae finished, her voice uneven.

"Maybe I could ..." He cleared his throat. They weren't allies. They weren't even friends. "Could keep an eye out. For the box." He supposed he could outright ask Foster. After what they'd been through ... he *would* ask. But Mae didn't need to know he had *that* kind of an inside line. She might use it against him.

Mae only nodded. Didn't say thank you, didn't say oh would you, how swell. She turned away and Jackson imagined when her hands went up, she was wiping her tears away so he wouldn't see. He was reaching for her when the window above the fire escape opened. A Chinese woman with a bucket of water stared at them.

"We —" Jackson reached for Mae's arm.

The woman shrieked and threw the water. Icy filth drenched them, carrying a stench Jackson likened to the bottom of a mereling tank.

Jackson pulled Mae down to the next ladder and the next and the next, until they were out of ladders and had to jump into a cart of fresh cut hay parked at the building's corner. They came up sneezing and coughing, but as they ran, prickly hay sticking to their wet faces and clothes, Jackson found himself laughing, echoing the sound pouring from Mae.

Sister Jerome Grace was waiting in Cressida's office.

Sister Jerome Grace was waiting in Cressida's office.

Sister Jerome Grace was ...

"Shut it."

Jackson stared at himself in the mirror, almost challenging himself to change into what he actually was, to not be the proper young man staring back. The shirt was soft from too much wash and wear, while the tie was confining, a hand closed around his neck. But Cressida said he should dress proper for the sister. He was surprised she stayed in the city, for he pictured her having already gone. It was easier to imagine she had gone on with her life while he tried to understand this new one.

He licked his palm and smoothed down his hair. He checked his belt, and his trousers, and his shoes, and everything was in its place. He couldn't see any trace of scale or shadow in the mirror so nodded at himself and approved.

Foster was not waiting outside Jackson's door as he sometimes did. Jackson knew his way around the building, though the corridors the public didn't traverse remained strange to him. The corridors connected every part of the building with every other, in ways Jackson couldn't understand. He found himself trying to map them in his head, but they were different every time, a branch that hadn't existed before, a fork that had once been a dead end. He trailed his hands over the walls as he went, swearing the building shuddered in response. Ridiculous. But then so too had those shadow figures been.

Pieces of darkness peeled away from other darkness. Surely he and Mae hadn't seen any such thing. Darkness flowing into a metal trunk as if it belonged there? Never happened. He tried to convince himself. He failed.

The door to Cressida's office was a beautiful thing. It was the same golden hued wood from the lobby, with an oval of frosted glass set into its center. Strange shapes infused the glass, changing as the corridors of the building did; there were often foxes chasing after birds, but sometimes these birds turned into dinosaurs and swallowed the foxes whole but for their tails. The door handle was wrought iron, always warm.

He knocked on the wood edge and sent a flurry of ravens up through the glass as he waited for Cressida to bid him enter. She did this in short order, expecting him, and Jackson stepped in to find her and the sister seated in the nook where Cressida received important visitors. Jackson's breath stuck in his throat when the sister smiled at him.

"Jackson." Sister Jerome Grace reached a hand out, beckoning to him.

Right now, it was only a hand, but he could imagine the palm split open, teeming with countless threads. He closed the door behind him and crossed the room to slide his hand into hers. Her hand was cool; Foster had told him earlier the sister was walking over, through the autumn sun and dappled leaves.

The sitting area was warm, a fire crackling in the hearth beneath the huge head on the wall over the mantle. Jackson could not say what this creature had been. From one angle, it looked like an ordinary elk, but from other angles, antlers turned into tentacles, the fur more liquid than it should be. Its eyes saw everything.

"Sister." Jackson sank into the chair beside the couch. He squeezed her hand then withdrew while Cressida poured from the steaming teapot at the table. Pastries sat on gleaming china plates: rounded puffs of dough oozing with cream, scones awaiting jam and cream of their own, and sweet almond cookies. The best china plates, perfectly white trimmed with gold ribbon.

He also saw, belatedly, it wasn't a table at all. The metal trunk from the docks sat there, under a crisp linen spread. He stared at it, mute, wondering if shadows leaked into the room or if he only imagined the fine black fog collecting around the trunk's base. Perhaps he was in his room, standing in front of the mirror. He willed himself to believe this, but couldn't get there. He drew his feet under the chair he occupied.

"Isn't this pleasant?" Cressida asked, but judging by her tone, she thought it was anything but pleasant. This only increased Jackson's belief the shadows were leaking from the trunk and that the sister's visit hadn't been planned at all, and ... He drew in a breath. A glance at the sister told him nothing. Her features were serene, as if nothing were amiss, but if they had been in the train yard before ... If they had been here before ... She knew what was to come? It was driving Jackson mad, not understanding how it could be.

Cressida handed the sister a cup and saucer, then poured for Jackson. Jackson didn't like tea, didn't *want* tea, but made no fuss when he was served. He wanted more soda, and wanted to get out of this room, before the shadows —

Did one just touch his foot? He gave a little kick.

"Jackson."

Cressida's tone commanded his attention and he tried not to fidget, but the weight of a sooty hand made itself known against his knee. Jackson saw nothing, but the sensation persisted. The hand squeezed his knee.

"Sister Jerome Grace is obligated by the church to check in on you," Cressida said, pouring her own tea. Her fingers tented on the teapot lid as she tipped.

Jackson listened to the gurgle of the amber liquid, but the weight of the not-hand on his knee kept intruding. He looked at the sister, who only smiled as if she couldn't sense a thing. Maybe she didn't.

"That isn't the only reason I came," Sister Jerome Grace said, her green eyes settling again on Jackson.

He exhaled, because he thought he might explode otherwise. The hand didn't leave his knee. It smelled of soot and brimstone, and was like a thing he had read about in a penny dreadful. It was awful, and he palmed his teacup even though it was too hot and should have stayed on its saucer.

He wanted to leap up and dance around to get the hand off his knee.

The pain of the hot cup gave him a place to focus so he wouldn't run away the way he had in Chicago. He told himself he was above running away, but it didn't seem so. Not with the sister so close and the phantom hand on his knee. Did they not see the shadows seeping like squid ink from the trunk? Did they not know?

Jackson forced himself to make small talk. "Are you s-staying in the city, then?" He looked from the bleeding shadows to the sister. She sat with cup and saucer on her knees, draped in her black habit. Hair yet hidden. Her expression softened at his question, mouth gliding up.

"For a little while longer," she said, "but I will see to another group of children on the trains. There are homes waiting for them in Chicago this time. Children from the shipyards here, going to work the lakeshore ..."

Children from the shipyards here. Black shapeless things until someone drew them from the dark with sounds suckering deep into his gut. Jackson lifted his tea, drank half the hot, overly sweet liquid. The idea of the sister tending to other orphans was like an itch in the center of his back. He didn't want there to be other children, he wanted there to be only him. He found this idea ridiculous. He thought he was happy here, but the sight of the sister proved otherwise. He pictured Sister Jerome Grace sitting on another train bench, holding another child's hand and his jaw seized up.

"It's an entire network you have, Sister," Cressida said as she leaned over the linen covered trunk to reach the milk pitcher. A shadow slithered beneath her black skirts and vanished. Cressida only tipped the pitcher over her teacup. Jackson watched it go creamy, white swallowing the amber. "How blessed are the children."

The second half of Jackson's tea was swallowed before he realized it and he reached for the pot, pouring himself more. He couldn't breathe, his tie tighter by the minute. The teapot made a clatter against the other dishes when he set it down. He reached for a plate and started filling it with cookies and scones.

"C-cream, Sister?" he asked, spooning the smooth clotted cream onto the side of the plate even though she hadn't said yes. She took the filled plate as he knew she would, and the linen napkin he offered her.

"Jackson has been fitting in just fine," Cressida said. Cressida leaned back in her chair, her cup and saucer cradled in her lap. Jackson might say she was nearly sprawled, one boot peeping out from the hem of her skirts as though her legs were spread beneath. Jackson watched another shadow vanish and his skin burned with heat.

Sister Jerome Grace set her teacup on the trunk, to settle her plate in her lap. She added a dollop of cream and jam to a scone and took a small bite, watching Jackson all the while. She chewed so slowly Jackson thought he might go mad. She dabbed the corners of her mouth with the napkin and only after she had placed it back in her lap did she say, "We knew he would."

Jackson loaded a plate for himself. He took mostly cream puffs, jamming them by the pair into his mouth so he wouldn't have to speak, so he wouldn't scream when the sooty hand on his knee hitched higher.

He listened to Cressida and the sister talk, but later couldn't relate a single thing they had said. When at last the sister was to leave, Jackson stood and the disembodied hand dropped to the carpet where it sat motionless. Jackson would have sworn it was watching him.

Only when he sank into the sister's hug did that sense evaporate. The circle of her arms sent every awful thing back a dozen paces, including Cressida. Jackson let his cheek rest against the sister's breast, he listened to the steady rhythm of her heart, and closed his eyes.

He couldn't say how long they stood like this. Time ceased to matter and he was back where he belonged. But when he opened his eyes, Cressida loomed near, silent fury masking her face. The sister's hand slid over Jackson's hair and he straightened, but it was Cressida's hand drawing him out of the sister's embrace at long last. Jackson couldn't bring himself to do it.

Jackson craned his neck, trying to get a look. The room was small and packed well beyond its capacity, the air sweltering. Every now and then, Jackson tried to catch Foster's eye, but the man wouldn't look at him, focused on the proceedings at the front of the room. They hadn't had a chance to talk since the dock and Jackson was beginning to wonder if it was intentional. He also hadn't been invited back to Cressida's office, so didn't know if the trunk remained.

The room didn't contain a stage, or dancers, or showy animals. A long much-worn table held an assortment of boxes, crates, trunks, and cases, each numbered. Two men oversaw these items, the younger assistant making a show of each item as it was described and bid upon. Jackson found it fascinating, as some of the items weren't described at all. One locked box sold for ten dollars, with no clue what might rest inside. People didn't seem to care.

Cressida placed the occasional bid, but didn't seem intent on anything. Jackson realized Foster kept an eye on a certain trunk, however. The red leather trunk was bound in brass and heavily locked. Given what Jackson had seen at the docks, he wondered. More shadows, or a different horror?

"Lot forty-two," the gentleman with the list said. "Red leather trunk, banded in yellow brass. Locks, keys, and two well-preserved heads."

A collective gasp rolled through the room. Jackson thought he had misheard, but the conversation burbling through the adults confirmed it. Heads. He moved under arms and elbows, until he reached the front and could see the trunk unobstructed.

The auctioneer unlocked the box and lifted the reluctant lid. The young assistant looked about to be sick as he put a glove on and lifted out a severed head.

It was ghastly, but Jackson couldn't look away. The skin was the color of whiskey, eyes tightly closed, mouth gaping in a scream. The cut at the throat was clean, though just above there was a faint mark, whether from a blade or a rope, Jackson couldn't say.

"A vicious bandit," the auctioneer said, reading from the list he held. "These despicable men come to you today to settle a judgment! Cutthroat and thief, renegade and pirate. They did little good in life, yet their deaths have eased the pain in countless hearts, and these funds will see those hearts further consoled."

Jackson didn't think Cressida cared about consoling hearts, but she did have an interest in the heads. She was not the first to bid, nor the second, but she made her interest slowly and firmly known. When she bid, one of the men dropped out, while the other stood firm, seeming not to care he was up against the Widow. When the price crested to twelve dollars, however, he cared. He shook off the auctioneer and Cressida was deemed the victor. She paid her money, had Foster collect the box and its key, and they departed.

Foster lashed the trunk into the automobile, then gestured Jackson toward it. "Your seat, *monsieur.*"

Jackson sat atop the box, holding it down on the drive back. Who in their right mind purchased severed heads? Then again, who in their right mind auctioned them? The closer they came to Macquarie's, the more Jackson realized he didn't care.

There was a method here even if he didn't understand it. Cressida didn't do anything without cause. Inviting the sister to tea in a room where a trunk filled with shadow monsters served as a table? Of course this had a purpose beyond its apparent intent. He thought back to the foundling hospital and how one boy there tried to befriend him with offers of candies and fresh socks. Jackson slowly to let the boy into his circle but quickly came to see the boy's actual target: Jackson's collection of penny dreadfuls. Two came up missing.

It was easy to turn the boy's eagerness back on himself; everyone wanted something. Jackson lured the boy into a deeper friendship, requesting more of his time, more of his attention, until the boy had only Jackson to turn to when something went wrong. Inevitably, something did go wrong; Jackson ensured it did. A misstep down a dark hallway, a turn into a room that shouldn't be there, getting tangled in what appeared to be cobwebs but became ropes that became Jackson's arms.

Boys went missing all the time, presumed to have run toward something better. There was never any sign of them in the hospital, so surely they couldn't be *there*, and they never returned. No blood, no bones, just gone, leaving Jackson to stack his penny dreadfuls into their proper place, the daffodil crate that brought him to the hospital.

He didn't understand everything Cressida did, but knew there was a layer beyond what he saw. Likely layers beyond even those, for what had Mae said? *The Widow controls so much of this city and she ...*

Not even Mae knew.

But Jackson thought he was getting closer. He was no longer a newcomer. He had seen it in Cressida's eyes when the sister hugged him. Cressida carried a secret that weighed her down and sucked her dry. Her eyes were hollow but for when she looked at him. And he was a part of this place now, a part Cressida did not want to lose. He knew if he proved himself valuable, it was only a matter of time. Time was one thing he had; he could feel it in the palm of Sister Jerome Grace's hand.

At Macquarie's, Foster gave him the trunk to carry. It was heavy, though maybe only because Jackson knew what it contained. They walked all the secret ways, deep into the building, to a room Jackson had not seen before.

The room was wood paneled from floor to ceiling, and contained no windows. A stack of trunks and crates occupied one corner, each draped in its own colored cloth. Some clothes glowed orange, others red, each flat surface supporting a collection of items. Small framed photographs, candles, coins and loose stones. The closer he got, the more he could pick out. A chicken foot, what looked like a human thumb.

"Here, Jackson."

Jackson kneeled with the trunk. He took the key when Foster offered it, but Cressida snatched it from his hand.

"Not tonight," was all she said before she swept from the room, leaving Jackson and Foster alone.

Jackson eyed the room. It was dreadful, long braids of hair filling one corner, small framed items on another wall. A tooth. A blackened nub. Two bones tied together with a black ribbon.

"This is her room," Foster said in a tone of caution, but he didn't stop Jackson from looking at anything. "We don't come here when she's in here. We don't do anything in here she don't ask us to do."

Another frame held a skewered butterfly, but there was no actual body, and only what looked like stretched skin in the place of wings. "What does she do in here?"

Foster shook his head, smoothing his hands over his tunic. "Haven't ever asked her. She does what she does."

The answer held no satisfaction. Jackson turned from the frames, to look closer at Foster. He didn't know how old the man was; despite the silver of his hair, he had an agelessness about him.

Old spirits, little Jackson, Cressida's voice whispered in his mind.

In her voice, he heard the call of train whistles even now. She was a thing he would never understand and almost didn't want to, for that would ruin the mystery. He envisioned some part of her here even now though he and Foster were alone, a Cressida-shaped wraith pouring from the walls like smoke. She looked younger than she ever had, despite the shine of silver whiskers against her cheeks; the meadows had come back to her eyes, the petals to her cheeks.

The smoke form kneeled before the fire and he watched as she opened an unseen bundle. He pictured crimson and cream fabric flowing outward from the small bodies inside. Three soft bats lay inside, along with three toads, and three spotted eggs. Somewhere in the room, shadows whispered.

Smoke-Cressida offered each item up to the flames, one by one, murmuring strange words. It was a language Jackson did not know, but took comfort in. He closed his eyes and rocked to the rhythm of it all, looking back to the flames in time to watch the eggs burst open under the heat. *Bat and toad and egg and oh spirits, come over me and into me and carry us away, beyond this place and time until we are ageless and everywhere and everywhere, like the rain, the rain.* The essence rising from the flames poured over Cressida, instilling her with a beauty and youth she did not naturally possess.

When he opened his eyes, this image was gone; only Foster remained, looking not at all surprised — had he seen Cressida this way before? Had she been here at all? Jackson's throat grew tight as the questions about the shadow creatures crept closer to his tongue. He tried to swallow, but couldn't, so asked. "An' what about those shadow things?"

Foster's head tilted and his eyes narrowed on Jackson. "Shadow things."

Jackson couldn't blame him for trying to see how much Jackson knew before he offered up his own information. As Jackson wouldn't give up that he had seen the transfer at the docks, he was certain Foster wouldn't tell him all he knew. Least not yet. "I am sure you will remember, Sister Jerome Grace came to tea the other day. In Cressida's office, there was a trunk … leaking shadows."

To Jackson's surprise, Foster smiled. "Everything in this place must eat."

"There's a thing in this place that eats them?" Jackson's voice fell to a whisper. He recalled the sooty hand on his knee and shuddered. Yes, those things should be swallowed, and then he remembered the gargoyles outside Bell's. The way the young boy had been upended.

"Would you like to see?"

There was only one answer. As eager as Jackson was to see, Foster was equally eager to show someone. Maybe it didn't matter who he showed; Jackson didn't presume himself special in that regard, but there was a familiar joy in Foster's eyes as they left the room and headed deeper into the building.

Foster took him to another elevator, one he had not seen. This elevator went further down than Jackson had any clue it could. The lower they went, the colder the world became and Jackson was thankful for his oversized coat. When Foster opened the doors, Jackson found himself inside a dark tunnel. Foster reached for a lantern and lit it.

"Don't usually have company down here. Gets so cold." Foster's breath fogged some in the damp air.

Jackson followed him into the gloom, through the close tunnel cutting through … The earth? Jackson couldn't tell how far down they were, but it smelled like dirt and the deeper they went, it smelled like the sea. The tunnel twisted around a corner and the air grew even colder, saltier. Jackson dragged a hand across the cobble of the tunnel wall and the dampness was gritty under his fingers.

"When the mister died, the ma'am was left all things." Foster's voice drifted over his shoulder in a fading poof of fogged breath. "Mister collected creatures from his journeys." Foster lifted the lantern and light shot down the tunnel ahead of them.

Jackson was reminded of the sideshow tents, of how something strange had been around every corner. This place was not so different, with the exception that he and the others were generally free to go where they would. The shadows had been boxed up, likely with good cause. Had the sideshow man told himself the same thing when it came to the snake woman in the cage? Jackson didn't like that idea right then, even if he understood it.

What Foster took him to was not a cage. The tunnel opened into a low ceilinged stone room with a broad pool of water spreading out from the lip of the floor. Jackson would have called it a swimming pool, but this was not so formal. The room had not been built so much as carved out, allowing the sea to flood it.

"The ocean?" Jackson made to step forward, but Foster held him back. Jackson saw the line scratched on the stone floor.

"Stay behind here," Foster said. He set the lantern on a metal table then reached for the nearby box. It was much like the metal trunk from the docks. Foster crossed the line on the floor and set the box at the pool's edge. He opened the lid and leapt back behind the line.

"Doesn't seem like much protection," Jackson said. "This line." He toed it. Nothing happened.

Foster didn't say anything. Jackson lifted his gaze to the box just as black vapor began to spill from it. It was strange how it happened; it didn't spill from the open lid, but leaked the same way the trunk in the sitting room had, from the bottom.

The color of the water in the pool began to change. At first Jackson thought it was taking on the black of the shadows, ink bleeding into the sea, but it quickly became something else, a large and shadowed form rising as if summoned. Two thick, black tentacles lined with suckers burst from the pool and landed on the edge, writhing no farther than the line marked in the stone. The tentacles pressed into the stone floor, to lift a massive body from the sea. This body was possessed of only one thing, a fang-rimmed mouth disinclined to hesitate before attacking the metal box. It had one demand: feed me.

It wasn't silent this meal. The metal trunk bent and crumpled as the beast chewed the shadows from it, the sound of rending metal causing Jackson to cover his ears even if he couldn't look away. When it wasn't tearing metal, it was screaming. Screaming shadows, screaming from a place Jackson did not want to envision. Water overflowed the pool, flooding the room, over Jackson's shoes and back under the metal desks and cabinets, but when at last the beast withdrew, so did the water, lapping back at the stone edge once more.

"Mister got that in Greenland," Foster said. "Thinks those shadows are its teatime." Foster gave Jackson a thin smile and Jackson shuddered. He thought of the sister and the table and the look in Cressida's eye.

"Was it a kraken?"

"The mister said so. You raise a thing in captivity, it grow smaller. You let a thing swim free … It fills up all the spaces it can."

For the first time, Jackson became keenly aware of the walls around them. Not only in the room, but Macquarie's as a whole. The foundling hospital had come to feel this way, too. It was a kind of captivity, a restriction. An inability to swim free.

Every Sunday, Cressida hosted dinner for her family and employees.

Not everyone came; many of those who worked for her had families of their own and preferred spending time with them. Jackson, however, wouldn't have wanted to be anywhere else, because the dinners became a slow pageant he loved to watch unfold.

Perhaps the building had once been a hotel, the formal dining room too large for the one table Cressida set. Every Sunday saw every chair filled. Cressida occupied the head of the table and while the chair at the foot of the table appeared empty, everyone said Mister Macquarie himself sat there, in spirit if not flesh. Water was always poured for him and sometimes whiskey. Some nights, a full plate of food was served. Some nights, it was said people noticed the level in the water glass nearby drop more than once, as if he drank from the world beyond.

Jackson never noticed anything in that regard, sitting directly to Cressida's left hand. The spot at the foot of the table was distant enough he couldn't tell what went on down there. Many times after a meal, if there was a smudge on a clean glass or the blue napkin was disturbed, Jackson never took it for the doings of a specter.

But tonight, Jackson wondered, because he watched the translucent dancers who flanked the chair and they laughed over things he could not hear. Small birds, not chickens or ducks, had been roasted with their heads left on. A fan of their strange magenta feathers had been saved to decorate their otherwise bald scalps.

Cressida pulled long strips of skin and flesh free to nibble as she would. Jackson found himself partial to the soda he got on these nights and the fried cow heels. He always found himself amazed at the quantity of food spread over the table and that very little remained when all was said and done.

"You honestly think the mister is down there?" Jackson asked Cressida around a bite of cow heel.

On reflection, it was the wrong thing to ask her. He might have asked Foster later when they were alone, or even one of the dancers. But to ask this question of the mister's widow was something different. Jackson's gaze slid from the empty chair to Cressida, who paused with a bite of bird between her lips. He had never seen such an expression on her face before. Not even the look she had given him at the sight of him hugging Sister Jerome Grace could compare.

Cressida bit the wing in half, returning the rest to her plate. Her hand slid into her lap where she clutched her napkin. When her hand came back to the tabletop, her fingers teased the edge of her unused knife. The silver edge reflected a line of light onto her fingers.

"You think I give a good god damn what anyone else thinks about the chair?"

Jackson set his half eaten cow heel down and took a quick swig of soda before wiping his hands clean. "That … wasn't what I asked or even meant, because I know you don't. Don't care. About — "

Her hand moved from the edge of the knife to cover Jackson's own hand. He went silent, half surprised the knife wasn't buried in his hand. Cressida smiled soft and her fingers stroked over the back of his hand in a slow rhythm.

Her voice was just as soft. "There are certain things I do care about in this household, little Jackson. I care about tradition and respect. I care about maintaining things as they are — respecting the way things are. One doesn't cross certain lines in this house, but you know this. You know this and yet …"

Her hand slid from his, to delve under the tent of her blue napkin. The next thing Jackson knew, two paper lions rested on the table between them. Hand-colored paper. Ivory ribbons. They smelled vaguely of mereling tank water. Jackson wanted to reach for them, wanted them back because they were not hers

Oh they were not hers

and his mind spun at how she had gotten them at all. He remembered his hasty undressing, kicking damp trousers into his hamper to get them off, not thinking about Mae's paper lions. Hadn't remembered to take them out, smooth them flat, and keep them where they would not be found.

"You do cross lines, little Jackson," Cressida said. She leaned back in her chair, more throne than simple chair. She sat a queen and Jackson a lowly petitioner, begging for something he needed to live.

"You didn't say not to explore."

Cressida's head inclined in silent agreement. "I did not, but I am certain Foster explained territory to you and how our business does not expand northward. North presently belongs to the Bells and until I can change that, I respect those lines."

She made the lines sound like little more than a nuisance, beneath even her notice,. Imaginary lines, like the lines he had drawn in the foundling hospital, but there even so.

"What did she tell you?"

"Tell me?" Jackson's hands itched to claim the lions; he held his napkin so he would not.

Cressida smiled. "I have given you a home, Jackson. You sit at my table and partake of my food." She reached for both fork and knife. She stabbed the bird's breast with the knife and began to shred the meat with the fork. The silver tines were merciless, turning the meat from a beautiful pale crescent into a ragged, frayed mess.

"She didn't tell me anything." He chose his words carefully, certain Cressida would know he was treading a fine line as were they both in this conversation. It was true, in a way, that Mae hadn't told him anything.

"Mostly, she wanted to know what I am. Probably so she can ... so they can ..."

"Defend against you," Cressida finished for him. She set her silverware down and a breath went out of her. "They have done such before."

Her voice sounded resigned now and Jackson sagged into his chair, thinking he had avoided one wound, but might yet sustain another.

"Did she try to tempt you into seeing her show?" Cressida touched the paper lions, a low rustle in the murmur of conversations around them.

"I went to a show, ma'am." On that point, it was best to be clear. Anyone could have attended the show, seen him there.

He thought this would upset Cressida, but the wound was in her smile, and the way she leaned back in her chair once more, as if everything had just fallen into her lap. "Oh, little Jackson. Maybe you are here for reasons even I don't fully understand yet. An inside line, straight through that young girl's ..." She paused, as if sorting words on her tongue. "... heart."

Jackson was encouraged to return to Bell's. At the discovery that his admission costs had gone up, he thought about telling Cressida, but decided against it. He knew as he stepped back into the theater and made his way to his usual place, he was willing to pay whatever cost to see Mae and her lions.

Cressida wanted information, she wanted him inside the enemy's territory, and would surely give him the money to get there, but it didn't sit right with him. He decided he would go because it suited his own needs, not because it suited Cressida's. He would tell her something — the number of people, the condition of the Bells — but she didn't need to know why he actually came. She already did, part of him knew. He told that part to shut it.

Tonight, the carousel women were dressed as mice and crows. The mice had soft gray coats, with large, colored ribbons tied around their necks. These ribbons echoed those drawn on the paper lions Mae had given Jackson; Cressida had not returned them and he had no doubt she knew what their loss would do to him. The lions were *his*.

Most of the crows wore long gowns of glossy black feathers; some of the feathers came loose as the women moved, to drift into the orchestra pit, onto tables. Others among the crows wore shorter skirts, lean legs turned violet under the drenching gaslights. Jackson sank into his usual chair and ordered a Coca-Cola when one of the crow servers sidled up to him.

The crows chased the mice, but sometimes the mice turned the tables and chased the crows. Some of the birds flew to escape into the rafters, and some over the audience itself. They were acrobats all, graceful and flying, and Jackson felt his want like a hard ball of sunlight in his gut. He wanted to fly, he wanted to possess the fliers, he wanted too much.

When Mae strode onto the stage, he wasn't prepared for it. Every show was different, he knew this from attending here and also Macquarie's, but this was something he had not seen before.

Mae wore a gown of starlight and pearls woven into white silk. It didn't seem like something a lion tamer would wear, no sheath of protective leather beneath the gown. There was only skin.

At her arrival, the mice vanished into the shadows and most of the crows went too. Only one remained. This crow, Mae stalked, without her whip until one of her lions padded onto stage with the curl of leather held in its mouth. Mae took the whip and the lion moved opposite her mistress, Mae approaching the crowgirl from another angle.

The crowgirl was careful with both Mae and the lion, allowing neither to get very close. Twice she escaped them by pushing herself into the air with her long black wings. As the lights flickered, Jackson could not pick out the wires that helped her fly, but soon didn't care. The entire scene shifted.

After the crow's second flight, the lion leapt forward with a growl and tackled the crow to the stage. There was no mistaking the scream from the crow, nor the snap of a bone inside that wing. Jackson's eyes widened, but he wasn't surprised when Mae flicked her whip to call the lion back. The lion stalked to her, pacing a line behind Mae, eyes on the wounded crow. Every line in the lion's body said it wanted to pounce, but it respected Mae's control.

Her control did not waver. The crow slid away when Mae approached. Mae's dress began to melt away as she went, skirts floating soundless to the floor, bodice falling apart pearl by pearl. The pearls dropped to the stage but where they went from there, Jackson could never have said. He was captivated by Mae and the ivory skin revealed bit by bit, even though she never came wholly naked. Shimmering starlight clung to every curve, galaxies and nebulae obscuring breasts and belly, hovering in a hazy skirt around her upper thighs.

The whip cracked as it curled around the crow's neck so Mae could haul her closer. Jackson, having experienced this on the roof, was transfixed. Mae made a silent gesture and the lioness leapt.

It was astonishing, the amount of blood spilled to the stage. Jackson wondered if it was wine or crushed fruit. At this distance he could not tell, could not smell it, but the audience reacted as if it were real. They stared in silence as the lioness ripped into the crow, as feathers exploded into the air and drifted back down. There would be vents in the stage, Jackson thought, to drain the mess away, a trapdoor a dancer could slide through to make it look as though only a husk of feathers remained.

When this became the case, the wings motionless, the lioness having gorged herself, Mae rose. Blood flecked her, starlight gone crimson. She coiled her whip, slid it into the lion's mouth for carrying, and both strode from the stage, as silent as they had come. Only then did the audience erupt in shrieks.

Jackson left his chair in the madness. Other dancers moved to clear the stage for the next act and the audience continued to holler in appreciation. He found his way to the narrow door behind a fall of curtain. He slipped into the darkness of backstage, where he had seen others go. No one paid him a lick of attention.

Backstage dropped into a half staircase, flanked by curving banisters and red-gelled lights so one wouldn't trip in the dark. Jackson was drawn to the low moan from beneath the stage. He followed the stairs to the doors nestled in their side, leading to the understage.

Mae crouched beside a bloody body. It was the crow from the stage; the blood was real, the body savaged by the lion, but the person, a male dancer, had not yet passed. On his other side, another woman crouched. She was older than Mae, brown-skinned, and held in her hands a sharp knife. She slid one hand into the ruin of the man's belly and came up with looked like entrails.

No. They were finer. Threads.

A jolt rolled through Jackson. His mind yanked him to the train yard with Sister Jerome Grace, her palm split open.

Mae's hands slid up the bloody threads as if feeling for something. A pulse, a knot. When she stopped, she looked at the other woman and nodded. The chest of the man between them rose and fell with ragged breath; the finery worn on stage was strewn around them, trampled, bloody.

The woman with Mae lifted her knife and drew it above Mae's hands.

This cutting was not silent; the man did not move so much as exhaled his last breath ever. Beyond that low breath, the threads crackled like dry twigs as the blade went through them.

Every hair on Jackson's body stood upright. The air warmed, like a hand against his cheek, and then was gone. The man on the floor did not move, the threads dead in the woman's hand. She drew her blade away and it sank into her hand the way Sister Jerome Grace's threads had.

Only then did Mae turn to pin him with her black stare. Jackson stared back.

Mae crossed his way. She bypassed him, to close the doors behind him. They had no lock, but Jackson could hear the ongoing show above them and had no doubt they would hear anyone before they arrived. Chances were, the following act wouldn't even employ the trap doors, because surely they knew about Mae. Knew what she was.

"You're fates." He spat the words, staring at Mae as she came back around him. His eyes darted to the other woman, tried to see the knife within her skin, but couldn't. "You're the other two." There was a relief in this realization, but his body also vibrated with unease. Had they all been here before? Or was the sister the only one who could draw a loop back around.

No — she said …

"I spun your thread," Jackson whispered, "and my sister could not bear to cut it … you have come to its end many times … *Oh*."

He wasn't sure where one thing ended and the next started. The room ceased to exist; he was moving before he realized it, changing forms, arms reaching for the woman who stood beyond Mae.

Everything was confusion. The whip snapped against his neck in a tightening noose, but he didn't stop. With a bellow, he charged the other woman and she *let* him catch her. He became very aware of this, that she let him, that she could have turned to threads and poured through his fingers, through the floor; could have cut this juncture, but something held her ... Something. Someone.

Mae.

This knowledge was like a rifle shot within the small room, puzzle pieces snapping into place. If this woman cut, and Sister Jerome Grace spun, it could only mean Mae determined how long a thread would be. How long a thing continued, or didn't.

He pushed the nameless one against the unfinished concrete wall. Mae shouldered into him from behind, a small warm mass that made him go motionless, but he did not surrender his hold on the woman before him.

She was like no one he had seen before, brown and round, black hair spiraling down her bare shoulders. She wore a costume of the theater, but was clearly no performer. Her eyes were not brown or black, but maybe sepia. When the light shifted, they were gold and amber, yellow like a watchful cat before they settled back to shadows.

"Why couldn't you cut it?" he asked and to his shame, his voice broke. He didn't fully understand this loop, the way the sister said they had been here before, but that threads had been spliced, tied.

He didn't expect her touch to be warm and gentle and familiar. There was relief in her touch, the setting down of a load he didn't know he carried. His shoulders straightened, even if his hold on her did not ease.

Her hand on him tightened, slid from his cheek to his neck, where fingers kneaded him as though he were dough. Jackson's eyes slid shut and a sound he did not recognize came from him, a low moan not pain, nor pleasure. It only was. He pulled himself back into his human body, so he might not feel the touch so keenly, but it didn't help.

"Because I couldn't bear it," she said. Her voice sounded like a bird call, a sapsucker's tap or a blue jay's demand, he didn't know. Then her hand did come away. "Some day I will."

In the motion, he smelled oranges. This scent clung to her, despite the death in the room, the body just steps away.

Some day she would bear it? Some day she would cut it? Jackson wanted to ask, but it was all he could do to open his eyes. Mae's whip slithered from his neck and he stepped away from both of them. Mae and the other drew together, then Mae stepped to the edge of the room, bringing a sheet of canvas over the dead body. They worked to wrap the body, plainly having done such work together before.

"Do you have a name?"

The woman's mouth twitched. "You may call me Beth," she said, and effortlessly rolled the body into the canvas. Blood stained the concrete floor, but she pressed her hands into it and drew it into herself.

Jackson half expected the body to vanish, for its ghost to bleed down from the ceiling, but neither of these things happened. Except for the show, the room held its silence for a long while as Beth and Mae worked to clean the mess they had made.

"You … So you …" Jackson tried to fit it together and couldn't.

Mae, who hadn't said a word since he had come down here, stared at him. She didn't look angry, but neither was she calm. Something roiled under the surface of her. "Every life has its proper length," she finally said. "There are proper ways to do things. For us, this is one."

Jackson shook his head. "No." He paced around them and while it was plain the blood *was* vanishing into Beth's hands, he chose to ignore it. "That's all this is, just another show, to pretty up what you did to that poor … person." It was an inadequate word, because the bird hadn't been costume, had been actual body. So were the others like they were, with multiple forms they could take and leave?

Mae tilted her head and an eyebrow inched up, as if she were waiting for more incredulity. Jackson decided to give her some.

"Probably just someone who overstepped their bounds, the way your brothers did in Chinatown," he said. He began to pace a slow figure eight pattern on the floor before them. "Everyone's got rules need respecting, and they weren't respected here. Little crowgirl didn't understand what she ... he ... did, or didn't care, the nuance to the situation likely didn't bother you any, girl who climbs up a fire escape to watch me in my room ... she doesn't need particulars, does she?"

If Jackson hadn't been looking at Mae, he would have missed the slight flick of her wrist. She and Beth moved in tandem, toward him as fast as wind. Beth's hand was fisted in his gut before he could protest, and a tangle of threads came around his wrists. Jackson screamed, but her knife flashed in her other hand, and she drew it down.

The world vanished.

Jackson, having been raised in the Catholic walls of the foundling hospital, expected a flood of white light. A chorus of angels with harps. Perhaps his mother and father would be there. They would inch forward and bend to their knees, seeking his forgiveness, which he would give without question, because this would be heaven, all would be repaired, perfect, without flaw. They would never know another pain. He looked, but there was only blackness.

And then, there was Mae and Beth and the tangled threads of his life. He tried to reach for them, but lacked hands or tentacles or anything that might touch anything. He tried to move, but he had no body to move.

"Everyone," Mae said, "has rules that must be respected. Didn't you just say that?"

He tried to meet her eyes, but either she didn't have any or he didn't have any, because he couldn't see her; there was only the slightest impression of her, the almost-garden scent of soap. Leaves and herbs and everything green. Beth was close, the smell of oranges not having evaporated.

"That includes us."

Mae moved as a whisper of breath on wind, even though there was no wind. He looked again for a source of light, for heavenly or divine intervention, but there was nothing. *Nothing.* He had difficulty understanding this. The sisters had told him and so too the fathers, so why was there nothing?

"Are you so certain you're dead?"

The essence of Mae's hand slid into Jackson's threads. It was base, the feeling shooting through him as her hand stroked up their length. She drew them out, untangling them with a hand that wasn't a hand, until the threads lay in perfect accord across the back of her palm. Beth came closer, blade resting in her hand.

"You aren't yet," Beth said, but she drew her blade across the threads and Jackson made a strangled noise as they came apart, as bits of thread frayed into the darkness.

"D-don't ..." Forcing the word out was like trying to breathe underwater. Jackson thrashed, but as more threads parted under her knife, a low whimper poured out of him, liquid and foul, and he hated himself. "I don't understand." These words came with more ease. "Don't send me away."

Beth's knife slid away and her fingers worked now, unhurried and true. She bound one thread back together and fused the ends of two others into one whole. Jackson didn't understand as he watched; he trembled in his own confusion.

"She won't send you away," came Mae's voice. "She doesn't make that choice."

Mae was the one, he knew, but there was something else in her voice, something —

Mae's face swam out of the dark then, a pale crescent, gibbous moon, waxing, waning, beautiful and distant, spilling light onto a million cities. He saw them all in this light and saw himself too, himself with Mae and Beth never far, but where had the sister gone? There was a hollow space where she should rest, a space Jackson didn't want to explain, though part of him surely already knew.

"It's like St. Nicholas," he whispered. "You cannot be this — you cannot visit and claim every person as they die ... How many people die every day? You cannot possibly ... You cannot — "

The blade emerged again from Beth's hand and the laugh that broke from him was ragged. If such things were possible, all things were possible and he was a fool for not understanding that.

It's only the understage, he told himself. They turned out the lights. We are there, and there is a dead body, a dead body only costumed because those can't possibly be real broken wings, and that body cannot have been disemboweled by the very hand that now holds ... That now holds ...

Here, the idea broke, because Beth's hand *had* been inside him. She held some part of him even now, her fingers cool and sure as if she were peeling the oranges she smelled of. He hated the idea that something larger than himself might be moving him around on the game board that was the world. Impossible. He had never balked at the idea of a heaven, but the idea of an all-powerful god —

"There is no one god," Mae whispered, "but only many, where — "

"I am not your plaything," Jackson whispered back, his voice trailing off in a hiss as the air in the room grew heavier. He felt like there was a hot stone on his chest. Her hand? His own atop it?

Something within him gave way. He allowed himself to be aware of this: the way his hand rested on hers, the way their fingers twined together, like threads themselves. He had no memory of touching her, of her not moving away, but there their hands rested. He allowed himself to relax, to understand what these hands meant. She held his threads, told Beth when to cut, but his hand rested upon hers.

When he lifted his hand, her own came away. The bite of Beth's knife eased and what had flowed out of him was once again swallowed and hidden. He understood the power in his own hand, and it made him quake with laughter. He did not feel like a fifteen-year-old boy. He was a man trapped within a body; he was a *monster*. He understood the monster in the depths of Macquarie's was nothing compared to him, understood even fates might be bent to one's own needs. Was it love that stayed Mae's hand and made her bend her own sister's in return?

As Mae's face moved from full moon into eclipse, he could not say. He could not crawl inside her mind and know its every curve. Could not fathom what made her or them act as they did. Sister Jerome Grace said he had to come here, and now that he was here? Did he have to stay? Or had he already been made into what needed making?

I made you what you are ...

The sister claimed such but here, Jackson refused that idea. She had not — he already *was* before her fingers set upon his threads. He had come from another place, had not been forged as humans were. He was something else, as were they.

The pressure of the air became too much. Jackson forced himself into motion, throwing hands and legs outward. He turned to move toward the door he knew was there — although it wasn't there, not until Mae's hand withdrew, not until Beth also curled away. The dark place they had inhabited vanished, the understage coming back to the fore, with its curled ropes, trap doors, and dead bod —

It was gone, the body and the bloodied mattress. Swallowed by that dark place or something else, he didn't know. He knew only the doors and their touch under his palms as he pushed them open. There were doors backstage, doors performers would open to catch a breath of air, to have a seat and smoke a cigarette. He flung these wide and stepped out into the world, a world that did not (could not) understand what he was.

He ran until his body refused to go farther, until his legs were weak and shaking from effort and his breath came in sharp, hollow puffs. Jackson fell to the alley street and heaved until he was empty, and then heaved a little more.

It didn't ease what was inside, the truth of him, the thing that needed expulsion. From some distant place, he heard laughter. Male and female and then gone. And he ached for that — to be normal in the night if it would have him.

Jackson didn't want to talk to anyone. Neither did he want to go into Kotler's Bakery the following day with Foster because he thought of the way Mae liked palmiers, and he couldn't not buy a handful of them himself if he went inside. Couldn't not imagine the way the flaky pasty would break apart in her mouth.

When Foster closed the door behind them, he was reminded of Mae closing the doors to the understage, and how her hand curled around his arm the way Foster's did now. Foster pulled him toward the gleaming bakery case, while Mae pulled him toward the slaughtered body.

Kotler's was busy, a variety of people filling the warm bread-scented space. Even so, the four clerks knew who Foster was and were coming to know Jackson. There was no wait for them. While Foster acquired bread, Jackson studied the pastries in the cases. The glass reflected his own image, the one place he looked like a normal boy — brown houndstooth coat with a crimson scarf the sister had given him. Christmas soon and he wondered if she would like a box of pastries for the holiday, though not the palmiers. Those were Mae's.

He bought five of them, the clerk wrapping them in brown paper before tying them with the standard blue Kotler ribbon. He paid, even though the young clerk shook her head, murmuring that their protection of this place was enough. The paper crinkled under his fingers and Jackson supposed Mae was not supposed to come here at all if this place was protected by Cressida.

This thought didn't trouble him as much as he suspected it should. He untied the ribbon and stuffed it into his pocket, unfolding the clever paper pouch as he and Foster stepped into the sun. The day was as bright as the understage, everything thrown into sharp angles with heavy shadows. The palmiers were filled with raspberry jam, and while sweet it carried a tart edge Jackson enjoyed. He glanced back, to the bakery clerk.

"Something wrong with the sweets?"

Jackson shook off Foster's question, looking beyond his own reflection to the girl behind the counter. She was pretty, in a perfectly normal way. She took pride in her work, carefully folding each packet for each customer. The way she looped the blue ribbons into bows was precise without being fussy; her hands simply knew the work.

He reached for the door, going back inside.

"What are — "

Foster's words were lost as the door swung shut. He made his way back to the counter, wanting to wait in the line like a normal person, but when the blonde clerk caught sight of him, fear widened her eyes. She looked from his face, to the packet of palmiers he held, and then back to his face. Jackson licked the crumbs from his lips and she took a step back, abandoning the customers before her. She vanished into the back room.

The other clerks stared at him.

He didn't bother to explain himself. He rounded the counter and followed the blonde clerk. None of the remaining clerks thought it out of the ordinary; they didn't follow, only turned back to the customers. Jackson found himself in the kitchen, a space that pressed hot damp fingers against his cheeks. A variety of faces looked up at him from their work: Chinese, European, but the clerk was not among them.

"Where did she go?"

He asked the question of a flour-covered woman beside a long counter. She had been kneading dough, but stopped to stare at him. Jackson wondered if she didn't speak English, but she nodded her head toward the back of the kitchen, and he found the clerk hiding behind the tallest oven, heat pouring over her.

Sweat beaded on her forehead and she pressed herself closer to the wall at his approach. Her eyes, blue like the napkins at Cressida's dinners, never left him. She held up one hand and it shook so badly he thought it might fall off. Where had the calm girl from the counter gone? She who could tie bows without so much as a waver?

"I'm sorry," she said and her voice was thick with an accent Jackson didn't know. She angled her shaking hand toward the packet of palmiers. "If you … If t-they're not to your standard …" Her fingers plucked at the brown wrapping paper, but Jackson didn't give up the pastries.

He wondered how she had been treated in the past to fear his simple return to the bakery. How had Cressida and her men kept this place in line? The clerks probably knew Mae, the family she belonged to, and what Cressida would say should she be found to be patronizing this place. These thoughts rained down on Jackson as the clerk tried again to take his bag.

"They're not …" Jackson's voice stuck in his throat and he took an abrupt step backwards so he wouldn't crowd her. He glanced at the others in the kitchen and saw they were all working, as though a young girl wasn't cowering in a corner.

"The palmiers are fine," he told her, hoping to ease her panic. "What did they ..." He couldn't ask that, wouldn't make her tell. "*Whatever* they did, I'm not going to. Just ..." It sounded awkward now, as the words rushed out of him. "Wondered if you might want to go do something sometime." He wouldn't take her to Macquarie's; he didn't think she would set foot in the place.

She stared at him, the hum and rattle of the kitchen rising up around them. As if to prove the palmiers were fine, he thumbed a complete pastry into his mouth, chewing while she thought about it. Her mouth twitched; surely he looked a fool with the pastry wedged in his mouth. It was almost normal, something a regular boy would do. Making a fool of himself in front of a girl.

When she nodded, he was more than a little surprised, but a spike of relief went through him. "Well, good then," he said and took another step back. She smoothed a hand over her face to erase the sweat. "I'll come by tonight."

She nodded again and Jackson realized only when he reached the street he didn't know her name. He glanced through the window again, but she hadn't emerged from the kitchen. Foster's hand claimed his arm — that scene under the stage rolled against him, beautiful Mae and that broken body and the way the Beth's knife had severed the threads. Jackson pulled out of Foster's grip.

"That isn't who I am," he whispered, and didn't answer Foster's puzzled look.

Her name was Gussie.

It was a perfectly awful name, she said, having belonged more properly to her uncle August who died the day she was born, bless his soul. It was the shock of her being a girl, everyone said with a laugh, but she couldn't help but wonder. Her family owned the bakery, she said as they walked along the docks. She didn't get to the water very often; her world was one of small warm spaces filled with yeast and flour and sugar. Her hands reflected this, creases yet embedded with flour though she had washed and changed into a fresh dress. There was a similar smudge of flour along her collar, but Jackson didn't point it out. Didn't even lean over and brush it away. He wanted to be tempted; he wasn't.

She was perfectly lovely in every way, from the fall of golden hair down her back to the bakery ribbon tying it back. Well-spoken when she realized he didn't mean to complain about the pastries even now, she accepted the sack of hot fried fish and squid he offered up. Jackson took his own sack from the vendor and they ate as they walked and talked.

Was this how normal people did it? He looked over the bay waters, the boats in their places, and wondered how many people came here just to watch the fishermen. It was quiet, the catch of the day already hauled in, taken away. It wasn't much of a place for a date, if this could be called that; it reeked of fish and salt, and the docks were slippery underfoot.

Gussie was all smiles, even as she gestured to the far island in the bay and its military prison. She loved to watch it, she said, because sometimes clusters of birds rose in huge clouds. They would wheel and soar and she wondered what it was like to fly. Lacking anything to say then, Jackson found a fried crab claw in his sack and offered it to her. She took it with a shy smile and looked away. She stopped walking then, freezing in her tracks.

Jackson followed her gaze to a group of three boys who approached. They were roughly the same age as Gussie and Jackson, and reminded him of the young men he'd fought in Chinatown. Jackson drew himself up, closer to Gussie's side, and when the other boys saw he was taller than them, their steps stuttered a bit.

"Got a new dog there, Gussie?" one of them asked.

Another picked the idea up with a laugh. "He's got you out for a walk, then. Be sure to clean up after her, aye mate? She's German. Don't know no better herself."

There came a shift inside him, the beast wanting to devour the threat. Jackson swallowed the monster, shoved it behind a door, and locked it in. If this came to an argument or brawl, he would take it the way a normal boy would. He would give the same way; there would be only fists, only feet.

"Not sure what your argument with her is, but leave off," Jackson said. He folded his sack of seafood closed and handed it to Gussie, taking a single step forward to place himself more between her and them.

The trio took a step back. Jackson was sure of his abilities even if he knew nothing of theirs. Fist to jaw, foot to gut, always mindful he had two hands, two legs, and could use both at once. But the young men continued to back up, shaking their heads now.

"Didn't mean nothing by it, did we?" one said.

Jackson cocked a brow. He started to shove his coat sleeves up his arms. Plain skin, no scale, and the idea he was holding that side of him away as the rage coursed was astounding. "Just thought you'd randomly insult the both of us, then?"

Jackson nodded and kept narrowing the distance between him and them. They continued to back up, shoes slipping in the wet muck.

"Reckon I'll just randomly bury my fist into three faces then. Fortunately, there are three right here."

The monster inside snapped, pressing against skin, but Jackson held it back, even as the boys turned and ran. He wanted to chase them, drag them down onto the dock and press them into the wood until they were the scum underfoot people slipped in.

Normal boys didn't do that. Normal boys blew themselves up to twice their size with chests out thrust and fists balled, and somehow it was enough. The trio didn't look back and when Jackson looked at Gussie. Her jaw was clenched hard. She handed the sack of fish back, still somewhat warm, then tore into the crab claw he had given her.

"I don't go to school," Gussie said around the bite of crab as if to explain. "My family needs me at the bakery, and that's more important than class. But they think ... Those boys think it means I'm ignorant." She threw the claw shell into the water and licked her fingers, not looking at Jackson as she reached into the bag for squid. "I study, just not with other kids."

Jackson didn't understand the fuss or the shame. He had never set foot inside a school, knew only the classes the sisters had run at the foundling hospital.

"And if you had been alone?" He looked again, to be sure they weren't coming back. It was too easy to picture those boys taking advantage of this place. Perhaps it was good she didn't have the time to come here. He wondered if she knew how to throw a punch, settle a foot hard into a groin.

"Suppose it would have been *me* running away." She looked around, then suddenly smiled. "Of course, I am a good swimmer, too."

Jackson smiled back at her and they walked in companionable silence. He took her back to the bakery; her family lived upstairs, in rooms too small and always warm, smelling like sugar or bread. She was certain her mother watched out the window to be sure she came home safe. Jackson glanced up and indeed saw a small face peering from the pane.

What was that like, to have someone worried about his return? When he returned to Macquarie's, everyone was wrapped in their own concerns.

Cressida didn't care he had been gone without explanation. Jackson went to his room and locked the door. He leaned there, wondering if he imagined the small figure leaving his fire escape, someone having waited for him after all.

It was with great caution that Jackson suggested to Foster they split their daily duties, to accomplish twice as much in half the time. If Jackson were allowed to take half the list and Foster the other, they could cover more territory and be done sooner. Foster, whose only affinity with numbers involved money and not time, was agreeable. Jackson knew the streets, and its people knew him. He was well respected where he needed to be, even if some elements wanted to try their luck against him, just to see what he could do.

Jackson didn't appreciate the reminder, because when they were out on errands it was easy to pretend he was normal. When they returned to Macquarie's, it became less easy. There were too many magical creatures, reminding Jackson of where and who he was. But he reveled in being alone, in going mostly where he wanted to, and when Foster agreed, Jackson took over the bakery runs.

Gussie soon grew accustomed to his arrivals and even began to slip him a free pastries. There were always leftovers, she reasoned, and if he didn't eat them, the birds would. Surely his belly would prefer them. Jackson never denied this and over the weeks, even the other clerks — her family, he had come to know — came to enjoy his presence. He supposed it was a doubly good thing for them: they had one of the Widow's boys on site if anything untoward reared its head.

The untoward thing was Mae and she didn't so much rear as she did outright leave. Jackson sprawled at what had become his usual place, the corner table by the window where the sun slanted in after eight. There was coffee and palmiers and today, Gussie was able to sit down after she had brought the order of bread for Macquarie's, because her cousin was also on the counter and they were not short-handed.

Gussie smiled a lot, took pleasure in simple things, and it was this Jackson tried learn. He told her about trying to buy a newspaper and how the newsboy hadn't understood him. It turned out the newsboy was deaf, which Gussie found amusing instead of amazing as Jackson did. He tried to imagine going through the world without hearing a sound and could not. Could a deaf person hear their own heart?

As he wondered, Mae entered the bakery. She was clad in a red dress, a bright drape of flame ignited by the sunlight behind her. Her hair was loose, her eyes strangely bright until they settled on Jackson and the laughing Gussie, the palmiers between them. The clerks called a welcome to Mae and looked anxiously at Jackson. He could have her thrown out; this was not her territory. But that wasn't why Mae stilled. She was above such things.

Perhaps she should have been above envy, too. Her lips parted, as if she meant to tell the clerks good morning, but then she stopped. Her skirts whispered against her knees. She pressed her lips together and the muscle in her jaw flinched. Her skirts hadn't settled by the time she turned back to the door. An older woman and her son were entering, but Mae easily bypassed them with all the grace of the lion tamer she was. Without a hitch in her step she was gone and Jackson was left with Gussie, who was laughing and hadn't noticed anything amiss.

Jackson curled his hands around his coffee cup then slurped at the black liquid. It was perfectly bitter, the surface rippled to hide his reflection.

He had not been to Bell's in twelve days. He was keenly aware of that lack in his life, even as he purposefully avoided it. Being normal meant not going to Bell's to see Mae or the shows. Not because of the pageant, but because he saw beyond all of it to the lie just below. Could see the women who were men, could see the costumes were actually skin and bone, could see the hollow understage where countless bodies were pulled.

Going to Bell's didn't make him feel normal. What he felt around Mae couldn't be normal. When he looked at Gussie he knew nothing beyond a curiosity to know what it was to be human. He thought if he studied her, he could be like her. He could cup his coffee like any man would and suck down the bitter black and not think of the wonders he had seen with Mae and Beth and even Cressida. Would not be forced to remember those creatures in cages at the sideshow; to acknowledge that surely there were other such places of misery for his own kind. His own kind was here. He was human, nothing more. Nothing more. Nothing. More.

It was a good and comforting lie to tell himself. Each night in bed, with the windows firmly latched against the intrusion he longed for (paper lions, coiled whip, the smell of her) he repeated it to himself. He was only what the mirror showed, a normal boy in a coat beginning to fill itself in from the hours of hard work. A normal boy who liked to read when he could and explore the city and … and.

Gussie was beautiful. Jackson leaned across the table and slid his hands over hers and wished with all his heart he might feel something for her. Her smile deepened as his coffee-warmed hands covered hers, but then she pulled back. Color flooded her cheeks as she tucked her hands into her lap. Perhaps it was too public, but he wondered at the idea of his mouth on hers. Wondered if she would taste pastry-sweet, even if he didn't care.

Beyond the golden fall of Gussie's hair, he watched Mae stalk up the street, her hands curled into fists. He shouldn't have cared, but he did. His stomach turned over and he wanted to go after her, but that meant not-normal, so he focused on his weight against the chair, on the hot coffee and the scent of Gussie beyond it. She smelled like yeast, normal and safe. When she returned to the kitchen, she briefly touched her hand to Jackson's. He didn't move, waiting for the shock of that touch to roll through him, waiting for something, anything.

All was quiet.

He stared into his coffee when she had gone, reflections layered one upon the other across its dark surface: the window, its panes of glass, its curtains, the edge of his own face. He tried to convince himself that Mae and Beth had done something to him, that in the understage, they transformed him into something that now possessed no hope of ever being wholly human, but every time he reached back into his memory, there was only that: no hope of humanity, because he had never been human. Would never be. Sister Jerome Grace understood, didn't she?

He left the bakery without a word to Gussie. The other clerks called a goodbye, and Jackson lifted his hand, but he was already moving beyond this space. Sister Jerome Grace. Sister Jerome would know.

The problem , he came to realize as he stalked south toward Macquarie's, was not knowing where the sister was. He slowed his steps, shoved his hands into his pockets, and glanced behind him. North, where Mae pulled at him as though he were a compass needle.

"Shut it," he whispered, but the feeling didn't go. It was as though every hair on his body stood on end and leaned north.

He walked away from her, going south when his body begged north, but when night inevitably came, he climbed to the roof. He gave in to north. He traced the path he knew well, over this catwalk and that drainpipe, until he could watch Bell's without obstruction. The desire to go inside was a sharp needle pricking against his skin.

He ground his teeth together, remembering what it was to master his different forms. This was no different, he told himself. It was learning to overcome and swallow the thing he always wanted to give in to.

The first time he changed it had been evening, shadows crossing the yard in long stripes. A boy stood in the corner of the hospital yard; Jackson could see him from his window and the boy was there when Jackson climbed down all the stairs, feeling as though he fought his way through a forest, though it was only an empty stairwell echoing with his footsteps. It was well past dinner and everyone was in their rooms, tucked where they should be, but for Jackson and this boy. This boy who stood with his face to the corner of the fence, hands clasped low against his belly, like he was holding his guts in. There was a gray scarf at the boy's feet, but everything had been gray in the evening light, heavy clouds having sucked the world of its color.

The boy turned and Jackson didn't know him. He wasn't from the hospital, for Jackson knew each and every child inside, having marked them well each time they dared come close. This boy was small and pale, and his eyes were constantly squeezed half shut, as if he had been kept in a dark place all his life. Maybe he had, because when Jackson drew closer, the boy smelled of rot, wet leaves. He crouched at Jackson's feet, as if he meant to pick up the scarf, but he never did. The boy seemed to dwindle, he was not a threat, and yet —

Jackson let the beast inside him spill from fingers and toes, until it swallowed his cloak of humanity. He would tell himself again and again the boy had been a threat, that his hands curled around the scarf and he stood, meaning to choke Jackson with the length of wool. Jackson would tell himself this, but would never believe it. Under the lie was the beauty of the truth, that Jackson broke him and swallowed him because he could.

There is no sin in being what you are, Sister Jerome Grace said. No sin in this, he told himself as he unhinged his jaw and chewed the boy to pulp. This boy who meant to attack him. This boy who had only wandered into the wrong yard, perhaps captivated by the rusting swings.

On the catwalk now, Jackson did not move, yet the metal creaked. He felt the weight of her body and came to his feet in a smooth motion, stepping backward as Mae approached. She didn't wear trousers, but the same red dress from the bakery. *Crescent moon in the dark of night and she means to kill me now, and be done with it, be done —*

Her mouth was sweet and it was rotten; it was the brightness of wet fruit and the dark of soaked mulch. Her mouth was the thing he most desired and the thing he should not have. Yet when her hands closed into his coat lapels, he did not refuse. It was clumsy the kiss, like learning to tie his shoes, like riding a bike down a steep hill, like throwing himself into boiling ice water.

When she pushed his coat from his shoulders, Jackson only stared. Mae pulled the coat so hard, the sleeves tangled, turning themselves inside out, bunching at his wrists. There was a little snarl from her, a sound that made Jackson laugh low. He took a step back and shook off her hands, if only to right the coat so it slipped from him to pool on the catwalk.

She pushed him then, hands hard on his arms, and not expecting it, Jackson went down atop his coat. There wasn't time to question her before she was on him again, straddling him, curling hands into his hair as she pulled his mouth back to hers. But mouths ceased to be mouths, became something Other Jackson could not discern, because it was too much.

He was not himself — or, was more himself than he had ever been, turning inside out under her hands the way she did under his. These human forms were only that — adopted forms, stolen in order to safely pass through the day. Beyond them, there were places — bodies — Jackson had never known, but was strangely familiar with. Hers was an alien world of hills and valleys, of clefts and planes, and he did not see the sunrise in her eyes, only the truth of an endless night, where they could always be whatever they were, refusing to cloak themselves in ill-fitting skins.

They had been here before — Jackson's not-hand slid down the curve of Mae's not-waist and he knew this place. The dip, the turn, the way she — *Oh, the way she.*

There was a thread, a cord of fiber and flesh pounding with a heartbeat. Jackson slid his hand up the curve that was Mae in the twilight of this in between place and lifted the thread, to feel its weight. It shifted in his hold, becoming so large he could not wholly encompass it even when he flowed his entire self into his hand. Its mass was impossible, but he rested this thread against Mae's mouth, surprised to taste the salt and heat of it against his own mouth. This thread had no immediate end. It stretched into the distance even as it hung against them both, moved with them, wrapped them.

When the world intruded, pushing city lights and cool air onto the metal catwalk, Jackson shivered. He drew his coat around them, a coat not oversized, but the perfect size, and perhaps it had been such all along, only waiting for her body to shelter alongside his own. Mae slid closer and Jackson wrapped around her, marveling at the way she had not flinched, had not only come to him but had wanted closer.

He dragged his hand across her sweat-damp hair, nestling his fingers against the nape of her neck where her pulse hammered. Where the threads moved inside her, even as they found a momentary calm. What was calm like, he wondered, for he could feel the thing inside him and it stirred yet. Wanting.

The blue door occupied a wall in the bakery basement. Past shelves of bagged flour and wrapped chocolate, beyond broken appliances, the door was nothing out of the ordinary. Its paint was so perfect it was hard to imagine anyone used it. The door's lock gave it away.

Jackson grudgingly admitted the lock was a true piece of art rendered in gold metal and etched lines, worn to a smooth shine from all the people who had touched it. People were the key — human people, Jackson understood, as Foster smudged Gussie's fingers over it. Gussie was light in his arms, even while trussed up, bound wrist and ankle and mouth.She made a grunt of protest. Jackson tightened his hold. According to Cressida, there wasn't much time.

It was surely the most disagreeable day in his history.

The vines etched into the metal moved under Gussie's fingers. The vines spiraled up and out, widening into flames before they burst through the top of the metal. The lock came unlatched and Foster reached for the knob, his hands carefully gloved. Even so, the metal caused his hands smoke, as though it burned him.

"What is that?" Jackson hissed. Gussie bucked in his arms and he gently shook her. "Shut it. Just be quiet and this will all be over soon — you don't even have to go with — "

Foster turned from the lock and reached for Gussie, hauling her into his arms, then over his shoulder. Her shoulder jammed into the black metal box strapped to Foster's back . Jackson stared and protested; Gussie was his last link to an ever dwindling world of humanity.

"Cressida said she didn't have to do anything beyond the lock. What —"

Foster strode through the doorway and Jackson refused to follow. But the lock had begun to knit itself back together, the door swinging shut under an unseen weight. He hurried through, his bones shaking when the door closed. The lock latched.

"She must come," Foster said. This was not apology, only fact.

In the small space, Foster's voice was very close. Jackson looked back, but couldn't see the door. Nor did any path seem to lay ahead of them. It was little more than a closet, until the floor fell out from under them. They did not plummet long through the darkness — it was more a roll from one space into another. Jackson was dizzy, unable to tell up from down until he became aware of spongy ground underfoot.

Everything was gray at first glance, but the longer Jackson looked, the more he saw. Logic told him they were only under Kotler's Bakery — in a closet, they had stumbled down some stairs, his mind tried to compensate even as he knew these things to be lies.

There had been no ocean journey, nor shadowed wood or glowing goddess with crooked fingers, only a locked door in the bakery's basement, but they found themselves in the underworld, rivers twisting in the near distance. Jackson bit the inside of his cheek, staring.

Five rivers were said to flow through the underworld. These five rivers spread through the whole of the known world, twisting like snakes back and forth upon themselves in the deepest hollows underground, sometimes swallowing each other, sometimes spitting each other out. These rivers joined in a great whirlpool moving with the sound of bones on bones. Jackson saw this with his own eyes and a frantic recognition rose within, even though he was certain he had never been here. He didn't want to be here now, but understood this was why Cressida had brought him. She needed him for *this*.

Near to hand was a waterfall, but the black waters flowed up and not down, as though the entire world had been tipped, and perhaps it had. The sky snowed ash, were it a sky and not the underside of the world, and winged creatures engaged in battle. Other figures on ground and in the water, all battling. For what, Jackson didn't know. Foster struggled over the writhing ground, carrying Gussie over his shoulder, ever toward the black rivers.

"Leave her!" Jackson hollered, but Foster refused. "Give me the girl or the box!"

Nothing was improved by having Gussie back in his arms. She stared at him, her blue eyes a furious misery. Her teeth tightened around the cloth Foster had tied over her mouth, and she growled — growled like she was a beast and not a human girl, and Jackson had to admire her. She bucked and didn't stop until he hoisted her over his shoulder.

"I'm not sorry," Jackson said, "even if I am." He was both things at once — not sorry because he and Foster had business here, but sorry because he knew what it was to be thrust into a world one didn't understand. Or want to be in. Jackson licked the ash from his lips, but tasted only Mae there. He hadn't seen her since that night — four days.

Foster trudged on. He was intent on the river, no matter the people who battled near its shore or in its depths. Jackson followed, the air growing damp the closer they came to the water. The ash stuck to his cheeks and eyelashes, but recoiled from the box Foster wore. The man looked as though he carried an invisible umbrella, so did the ash avoid him.

The people at the river were not living people, nor monsters; they were the undead. Some had coins in the place of eyes, while others carried coins in their mouths. Some had no coin at all, but all were trapped where they stood and so chose to argue about it. Some waded into the water, but were quickly consumed by the soft ground, swallowed up as though they had never been. As one was swallowed, the level of the river rose, bleeding farther across the spongy ground.

Foster stumbled, sodden shoes catching in a spongy loop on the ground. He went down hard on both knees, the box he carried slamming into the back of his head. Jackson lunged and Gussie took advantage to buck out of his arms. Jackson couldn't hold her; she joined Foster on the disgusting ground. Jackson stared at the two of them in bafflement as the undead wandered silent and slick with wet ash.

"This ..."

Foster's voice was only a rasp, a sliver of itself. He lifted a hand, a hand beginning to go green around the edges. He reached backward, but his hand closed on ashen air. The ash did not cling to him, but once lifted his hand collapsed in on itself, flesh buckling as though sucked away. Jackson could see the hard outline of bone under the tautly pulled skin.

"Fos — "

"This!" Foster's hand was wet slop when it connected with the metal box he wore. Blood and melting muscle smeared the side of the box as his arm fell to his side.

Jackson ignored Gussie's wriggling — the way she was tied, she might get a few feet, but no more. She was not melting or turning green around the edges. Jackson moved to Foster's side, kneeling to untie the rope that held the box to the rapidly melting body.

"This ... will stop him," Foster whispered through his ruined lips.

Jackson pulled the ropes away and the box rolled into his arms, to rest heavy against his chest like a small child. The box shrieked the closer Jackson got to the river and then he knew. Shadows. Foster meant to call the kraken. But what might that beast do here?

He hesitated, looking back at Foster. His body looked more like a melted candle and Jackson stood torn between doing this thing and saving his friend. Scooping him up and carting him back to the bakery basement. But the look in Foster's eyes was resolute. This must be done, so Jackson staggered over the spongy ground until he reached the river's edge.

He did what Foster had done in the room below Macquarie's: he set the box in the water and pried its lid open. When the blackness emerged, it came again from the bottom of the box. Jackson did not move away before one of those awful shadow hands slid up his own leg. Here in the water, the seeping coldness of the creature held an electric shock. It would swallow him, and perhaps did carry a piece of him away before he kicked the hand and skittered away from box and beasts. Did they laugh? Jackson would have sworn it was so.

The blackness did not have long to wait. The water had never been-motionless, churned by the restless ground itself, but now, something new spurred it to motion. It was as if the very water itself wanted to crawl out of its hellish banks, to escape the thing crawling from the depths. The ground vibrated with its approach and though the wandering undead looked, they never ceased moving as if in concert *away* from the shore they had once fought so dearly to reach.

The kraken came with an obscene speed, bursting from the river to send black water inland. While it claimed the box and its inky contents, it also seemed keenly aware of what it was; its massive eye looked around, as if for a danger Jackson had not yet perceived. Its tentacles and arms writhed in the air to deflect any incoming attack. It was then Jackson realized what a fool he was. Why bring the kraken here to feed it only shadows? There was something else.

The something else came from the heart of the ebon whirlpool. It appeared no more than a man, for this figure possessed two legs, two arms, and an upright body. But as it neared, pulling itself through the air as though air were a corporeal thing it could control, Jackson saw otherwise. This figure was black as night and its head was insectoid; from its shoulders, the head rose as a gleaming black carapace. Wings spread outward from where his cheeks should have been, vicious mandibles snapping the foul air.

The kraken enveloped the figure with one long tentacle. From toes to chest, the man was wrapped as he emerged from the water, dragged closer for inspection; the kraken did not blindly shove this man into his mouth. There was a curiosity, perhaps a respect, which sent a chill down Jackson's spine. The kraken knew what the man was about and weren't intelligent monsters the worst?

The insect man was not alone; two women came to his aid, these painfully known to Jackson. He stared as Mae and Beth flung themselves into the fray. None of them stood a chance — the kraken was the size of three mountains in this place, writhing and black and the worst thing Jackson had ever seen. Yet when Mae touched it, the beast released a bellow like none Jackson had heard. Its flesh shuddered, the way the ground did with an earthquake. Mae carried her whip, and Beth her knife; the whip lifted the beast into the ashen sky, Mae pulling until the entire length of kraken was freed from the river.

Wet tentacles lashed the air; the air itself was marked by their passage, gore streaking the sky. They lashed Mae and Beth, too, enveloped them, and soon the women were coated in blood, slime, and the muck of the river. Their cries carried in the damp air and from the wet darkness loped a dozen lions, as if responding to Mae's call. They went no farther than the riverbank though, flinching from the touch of the water.

Jackson pushed himself to his feet, having no idea what he thought he might do. They meant to kill the kraken because the kraken meant to kill that man — the man who controlled this underworld.

And Jackson stood weaponless. He had called the kraken to this battle, and now … Now.

There was no choosing sides; it was instinct that drove him to call the monster inside himself, to change as he never had before. If the kraken was the size of three mountains, so was Jackson. Knowing only the need to do it, Jackson hit the kraken head on, tentacles wrapping over tentacles. Jackson sucked every whipping length inside his grip so Mae's whip could tighten on the kraken's head. The whip had left a scar, and Beth's knife gleamed with the brightest light in this land as she drew where her sister had marked.

The blade sliced through the flesh as though it were only air, the kraken coming apart piece by piece. Jackson pulled more tightly until severed tentacles fell into the river. The water boiled beneath them, as the massive kraken head deflated within the circle of Mae's whip, of Jackson's coils.

They all tumbled free, shrieking at the touch of the river as they landed. The water was scalding, fire and ice both as it ate away at Jackson's scaled flesh. He was a trembling wreck when he reached shore again, half boy and half beast.

"Mae."

She hauled herself to her feet amid the roaming undead who lingered at the riverbank. All was confusion, until Mae reached for the nearest person and drew her hand into their guts. The world moved again and Mae cried, tears tracking clean paths through her filthy cheeks. Jackson didn't understand, not until Beth came with her knife and cut the threads. Not until the insect man hauled the body close, and into the boat resting on the shore. One by one, they tended the undead, cutting the threads and filling the boat.

Doing the work they had been unable to do because of the kraken.

§

Jackson hauled what remained of Foster from the ground in his own coat. He was not wholly gone and Jackson had some measure of hope he would come back to his proper self on the other side of the door. He kept Gussie tied until they reached that door, then pressed her grimy fingers over the locking mechanism again. The door unlatched with a soft click.

Jackson stuck his foot in the door, as he untied Gussie with surprisingly steady hands. The rope binding her was slick and the work was slow, but he suspected it was easier than the task left to Mae, Beth, and Charon. The undead on the riverbank only multiplied as they cut threads and ushered people onto the boat. The waters had calmed and Charon poled across the river as easily as Jackson drew breath.

Gussie ripped her hands out of Jackson's grip and waited until he removed the cloth around her mouth before sinking her slimed fist into his face. He grunted and staggered into the door, pain exploding from his left eye, down his nose, and into his jaw. Without thinking of the muck that covered him too, Jackson pressed his hand over the flaring pain, and got a nose full of the underworld for his troubles.

"God fucking damn," he muttered and let his hand fall away. He stared at her, but had nothing to say. If this bakery were her family's own, and they welcomed Mae even though Cressida's protection said they should not, she knew damn well what the basement held. All this time.

He said nothing, but pulled the door shut as he headed back to the underworld. He would worry about getting out later — if it was a human touch that unlocked the door, there were plenty of humans left on the riverbank. He would worry instead about all that was to come before he left the underworld. He and Mae and Beth had slaughtered the kraken and he felt sure this was not what Cressida meant when she sent them on this mission.

The undead troubled him, but not so much as the living on these banks. He approached the scene slowly, unable to ignore the care Mae and Beth and even Charon took in their work. The people wandering the river-bank had ended their normal lives, but a journey remained ahead. They were people from every walk of life, the poor and rich alike. The work done by the trio was almost reverent, threads drawn out of each body, measured to the perfect length in Mae's hands before Beth severed them. Charon, like a portal of darkness at the end of the line, helped each person onto his boat. Sometimes there were coins. Most times there were not.

How long had these people waited? How long had this work gone undone? Why had Foster fallen to pieces? Jackson's gaze came to rest on Mae as she worked. He wanted to ask, but it was strange to speak in this place of the dead. Speech was a thing for the living. Even so, Mae's eyes found his and there was a trace of a smile on her mouth when she broke the silence.

"Some are not suited to the underworld," she said, drawing another length of threads out. "Foster's kind is acquainted with acquisition, not loss. He cannot give any part of himself to this place, so this place takes what it will, without thought."

The weight of questions rested between them. Mae nodded, as though she heard everything he didn't ask, but kept to her work. Jackson didn't press. The crowd dwindled, the undead calming and wandering less. Those who had not been here so long, Mae told him later, would not feel such a need to cross the river.

Charon was pushing another full boat across the water when Mae at last let herself rest. From shore, Charon's lantern sent eerie patterns of light across the stirred waters; the ash continued to fall, sticking to everything, yet never accumulating.

"There's things to talk about," he said as he dragged his hands across his cheeks. A layer of ash came away and he flung it to the ground where it landed with a wet slop.

Mae wrapped her arms around herself and Jackson thought to offer her his coat, but only then realized he had used it to transport Foster back to the other side. The longer he watched her though, he couldn't tell if she was actually cold. Maybe she just longed for arms around her. He didn't move, uncertain.

"Plenty," Mae agreed and pulled her attention from the water. "The kraken — "

"Was Cressida's. Saw it in the cellars with Foster one night, watched it feed. Don't know how this place connects though?"

"Water goes where it will," Mae said. "And these waters wrap the world, so why wouldn't it connect? Everything is tied together if you trace the line back far enough."

She tilted her head and Jackson noted the exhaustion in her eyes.. What was it like, he wondered, to hold all those threads and determine where they should be severed?

"The kraken prevented us from doing the bulk of our work. Gussie tried to help, but there was just too much. Death never stops."

Jackson nodded, wiping more ash from his skin. It was bothersome and cold, like jelly as he swept it away. "Cressida did that then." It wasn't a question, but Mae nodded.

"She offers the bakery protection, so feels the protection extends here." Mae looked around the gray world in which they stood, the light upon the river having dwindled to a pinprick. "Surely you have seen the things she does. It's more than just territory with her. It's the attempt to live forever, to stop death, despite the fact that I already know when her threads will be cut."

Jackson didn't ask when. He could feel the knowledge resting like a warm hand against the back of his neck, the way Cressida's own had done countless times. He thought of the heads, the strange ritual room, and nodded, having no other way to explain these things. He knew and he pushed the knowledge away, closed it behind its own door. Later, he told himself.

"She strengthens her hand against fate itself," Mae continued. "She adopts the strange in the world, training them to fight for her against all reason."

She reached for him then, her ash-wet hand sliding against his. It was electric, twice as painful as the touch of the shadow creatures. Jackson did not move away from it, but wrapped his hand around her own.

"She saved me from a life lived behind walls," he said. His throat had gone tight, but from the contact with Mae or the memory of the hospital's walls he could not say.

"She did," Mae said. She lifted their joined hands, smearing more muck into his palm. "This will open the door for you."

Jackson's lip curled a little as the realization of what the ash in the air was hit him. The remains of all those lives. He looked beyond Mae, to Charon who helped another person into his boat. "Where do they go from here?"

Mae glanced back, too. The more recent arrivals were more reluctant to hand their coins over. Jackson wondered what Charon did with the coins, what Foster would make of them if he could tolerate this place.

"Across the river," Mae said, and her voice had gone softer than Jackson had heard it yet. "I don't know what lies on the other side. It's not for me to know. Beth knows and never speaks of it." She looked back to him, her expression grave. "Sister Jerome Grace doesn't even know of this place, for she is the start of all things, not the end. Go tend to Foster now, hmm? And Gussie."

Jackson never believed he should apologize for his friendship with Gussie — perhaps because it now lay in tatters, a thing that would never be, or perhaps because he now understood Mae's anger at the sight of him with the human. It had been about this place, not about holding hands and sharing pastries. Hadn't it? Was it possible Mae longed for what he did, a life lived normally?

He leaned in, to kiss the ash from her lips, and somehow beneath all the bitter, she remained sweet, tasting like jam-filled palmiers. Her mouth tipped upward under his and then she was gone, back to her work with the dead.

The walk to the door was eternal. The ground always gave too much underfoot. When Jackson allowed himself to become what he was, he found he moved with ease, viper coils slithering over the sponge without stumbling. Foster and Gussie remained in the small closet-like space, crouched. Gussie's knees were drawn to her chin and Foster was more solid and less green. The idea that Cressida sent him here was like an ice water dousing for Jackson. Foster was Cressida's closest confidant. She had risked his loss in order to secure this place. Conversations to come nibbled at the edge of Jackson's thoughts like fish with slippery mouths.

He slid his ash-smeared hand against the lock mechanism and the door notched open. Gussie was through it in a flash, but she didn't flee the basement. She lingered by the shelves, dripping with goo, her arms wrapped around her shoulders.

"Not going to apologize." Foster slurred through his misshapen mouth as Jackson lifted him out of the room and into the basement.

Jackson slid his filthy hand back over the lock to close the door and watched as the metal consumed the ash and muck. When finished, the metal gleamed. He looked at Foster and then Gussie and nodded.

"Doesn't seem to be a thing to apologize for."

"How about kidnapping me?" Gussie asked. Her blonde locks dripped with underworld muck, splattering the floor in a ring beneath her. "How about tying me up, gagging me, and forcing me to do your — "

"I asked nicely," Foster said. "That did not work."

Gussie's chin lifted, but she said nothing. Her blue eyes might have burned holes through Foster and Jackson both had she been anything but human. Jackson's hand slid cautiously over Foster's shoulder.

"Can sit here 'till you're up for walking."

Foster nodded, wobbly and not entirely solid. Jackson helped pull his coat around Foster's bent shoulders, then looked to Gussie.

"How long's Mae been coming here?" he asked.

Gussie shook her head, then shuddered when tendrils of her hair stuck to her cheeks. More goo dripped onto the concrete floor. "I can't remember her *not* coming here," she said. "She's always been."

"And Cressida?"

There was another shudder when Jackson evoked that name. Gussie's arms curled more tightly around her and he saw she was crying; the salt in her tears rose sharp in the room.

"She's always been, too. Mister Macquarie, he ..." Gussie's throat worked as she swallowed hard. "He tried to make peace, but it couldn't be done. Charon said the work... The work won't end, and we're...we're just on top of it all, and — T-that's when Mister Macquarie brought the ..." Another shudder; she couldn't say the word and Jackson wondered what she had seen of it before, what the kraken had done in prior attempts.

"Kraken," Jackson said. The beast he'd had a hand in seeing killed.

He looked at Foster, whose jaw was set firm. "Cressida meant for it to kill them once and for all." It wasn't a question, just a statement of fact, and when Foster nodded, Jackson stood relieved. He liked this man, the way he was unapologetically himself.

Gussie moved from the shelves, shuffling her way toward a stack of linens. She brought towels, though Jackson had forgotten the muck he was covered in, focused as he was on where he needed to go next, where he needed to get Foster. When Foster could get his legs back under him, Gussie took their towels and stared at them from eyes gone hollow.

"W-what happens now?" she asked.

"Need to talk to Cressida," Jackson said, and saw the panic well up in Gussie's eyes to fill all those hollow spaces. "She won't move on this place again."

Taken as a whole, they were big words from a still-young man. He wasn't sure how, but he wouldn't let it happen. The lines as drawn could not hold. The walk back to Macquarie's took a lifetime; Jackson expected them to shuffle in as old, gray men, not the muck-damp things they were. In the entry, Foster buckled to his knees, coughing. Gold spilled from him, some of the coins given to Charon. They both stared at them in bafflement, but picked them up nonetheless, hiding them in pockets as Cressida approached.

At the sight of her, the darkness within him unfolded, but he held it back, just beneath his skin where it served to fuel his anger. He couldn't have this conversation here, not when they were just inside the doors, but Cressida knew that, too. With all the care of a human mother, she bundled Foster against her side and guided them both into the depths of the building, to her office.

The glass flared with rioting hell horses, black amid the frosted pane. Jackson swallowed the shudder he felt; if he gave in to that feeling, he would slip from one skin into the next.

Cressida saw Foster settled on her sofa, pressing him gently into the pillows and drawing her tea set close. She poured for him, a thing that had never happened, and pressed the steaming cup into his unsteady hands. She held him for a breath longer, then withdrew, to look at Jackson. Gauging. Saying nothing.

"Don't drink that tea," Jackson said.

He didn't know, couldn't be sure, but Cressida knew when things went her way and she knew when they did not. And if she had been willing to risk sending Foster to the underworld, why wouldn't she move against him when he failed in this thing?

She went still. It was small, considering all that followed, but Jackson would remember it. Would remember the blankness that moved across her green eyes, only a surface thing, transient. She blinked and came back, to the realization that things had shifted.

"Don't be foolish," Cressida said with a laugh, even as Foster leaned forward and set the cup down on the table — the table that was a table now, no longer a metal box filled with leaking blackness. "Tell me what happened, is all secure?"

He felt small in the close room, as though the walls were retreating, to leave him and Cressida alone in the dark. She was telling him to be himself and punishing him for being that very thing. Now, with each breath he took, Jackson allowed himself to be more of what he was. It started with his feet, shoes long since lost to the underworld.

"It depends greatly which viewpoint you use," Jackson said. His feet vanished in a rush of black scaled skin that turned itself inside out as coils erupted across the carpets. "My viewpoint is this: the bakery, and what it contains, is secure, because you won't touch it again."

He was so small, the floor seeming to crumble beneath him as Cressida rose from her chair. Foster fell into the blackness with the walls, parts of the world receding because he did not need them. Needed only himself and her, to …

To what?

"You dare question my reach?"

Did he? "You claim to respect lines — "

Cressida's laughter cut his words off. Her hand slid over his, sudden and warm, the sound of rustling beetles. "Until I can change them."

The first snap was like a twig, a sharp scent of sap rising in the black. He wasn't sure what it was until he saw the queer way his smallest finger dangled, broken in its fleshy guise. The pain was liquid and hot, rushing up wrist and forearm. It hit his elbow and then the second snap, another finger broken in Cressida's hold. Jackson buckled, pain stealing his focus. He was going to — Do something. Move something. Change something. But now …

His hand was on fire, Cressida breaking bones one by one. He screamed and there were words, but they were incoherent. Hers came through, condemnation.

"How dare you? How dare you forsake this? Our house, our home. Our *family*." Her voice trembled on that word and through the pain Jackson didn't know if it was honest or not. "Such a tiny thing that no one wanted because you were too strange. Because you changed in the night, soiled your bed with things you could not rightly explain. Little box boy no one wanted. Only me."

She moved like fire through splintered timber, inhuman then, drawing on whatever sources she could call to hand. The hell horses in the door burst out of the glass, troops rallied to her cause. With a scream, Jackson shifted forms, forcing his broken fingers away, so the blackness might writhe from him. But even these parts of him were broken, aflame. He reached back with one tentacled arm to sweep the horses to the ground. They shattered into glass fragments.

Cressida countered with a small metal box. Jackson lifted his hand again, to sweep it away too, but brightness burned from the box as she opened it, and he could only stare.

There were no shadow creatures, when Jackson would have welcomed them. His breath left him when he gazed on the severed hand that rested on a bed of straw. It looked small there, not blue or pale the way it should be, but flushed with the color of life. The fingers were bent inward toward the palm, where it held a golden cross. This cross gleamed at Jackson, showed him his own reflection back again, showed him all he could never be — told him to trust all he was.

If Cressida had thought the hand would be his undoing, she was right — but likely not in the way she expected. Jackson's human form fell fully away as he embraced himself in a way he had not yet. Though he was weak-kneed and broken-handed, he did not crumple to the carpets and sob for Sister Jerome Grace. If she had known he had to come to this place, she knew this place contained this point in time. If she did not know of the underworld, surely she understood that all things created come to an end.

Jackson moved with thought and instinct both, taking Cressida into his broken, writhing hands. She was bubbling soda, her own skin giving birth to something Other, but this never fully came to pass. There was that fizzy feeling, the near-eruption, but Jackson's hands on her kept her from finding that form. Jackson shoved her into the floor, the metal box tumbling away. He wrapped his hands around and around her throat, until she gasped for breath, until she pleaded.

"Don't — "

Jackson forced the question past his misshapen mouth, grip never easing. "Why would you take such a thing from this world?"

She struggled to free herself from his hands, but could not, and laughed even so. "If I cannot have eternity, why should *anything* be born? She abandoned you to this awful world. I chose you! I chose *you*!"

If things could no longer be born, things could surely still die. Jackson did not release her. Not when her eyes rolled back. Not when her mouth gaped for air like a landed fish. Not when she thrashed and then went terribly still. He held her tight and tighter until there was a touch on his shoulder, and another touch on his hand. He was aware of Mae and Beth, even if he didn't properly see them. They were a whisper of air as threads were drawn up and out, as Mae measured and Beth cut. Jackson could not say if he imagined the glee in Beth's eye at the cutting of these threads. It tasted like broken orange slices against his tongue.

Neither Mae nor Beth tried to uncoil his hands from Cressida, but neither did they leave his side. They vibrated the way dragonfly wings did in summer air. When at last he could relax and pull himself from the body, he brought himself back into his human skin, too. In tattered clothing and shivering, he crouched before the metal box and drew it close. The sister's hand rested there and as he watched, countless threads unspooled from the severed wrist. Innumerable. Growing. Breathing.

§

He left before anyone could talk him out of it, heedless of anything but the need to get away. With his ruined hands, he drew his suitcase from the shelf and carefully opened it. Every motion was agony. One change of clothes, one metal box, spare shoes. He couldn't fathom ever tying shoes again, but wouldn't leave them. He found it strange when the metal box holding the sister's hand fit into the suitcase perfectly. As though one had been made for the other.

The halls of Macquarie's stood quiet. He clutched his suitcase against his chest and paused in the darkened lobby, listening to the building breathe — he pictured it as Foster's breath, the deep and regular sounds of a body repairing itself. What became of it was not his concern and yet he found himself reluctant to go. He thought of the performers here, told himself he didn't care. Even as he walked the dark path to Cressida's office, he told himself he didn't care.

He closed himself into the space where she had died

(where he had killed her)

and closed the door behind him. The broken glass was empty, all creatures flown. He liked to imagine they had been released, and were in their proper places now that they were no longer trapped in the glass. He didn't know, but he liked to pretend.

He went to Cressida's desk, opening the drawers one by one. He didn't care for most of what he saw — it didn't matter, not even the small dried krakens she had strung on a rope of pearls. They weren't what he sought. Neither was the box of gold coins and carefully stacked bills, but he wasn't above taking these, understanding he would need them if he meant to make his way in the city. In the world.

What he truly sought had been pressed into a book he found atop the shelf in the sitting room. He pulled the book down with a shuddering cry at the pain this caused his hands, and opened it where the ivory ribbons spilled. He drew out the paper lions, carefully smoothed flat once more, and kicked the book away.

He left before he could talk himself out of it. He knew the city forwards and backwards, but it remained an alien thing tonight, no moon above to light his way. He opted for Chinatown, disregarding the way his heart tugged him north. Perhaps the territorial lines had been erased with Cressida's death, perhaps they hadn't. The Bells would do what they did, as they had always done.

Chinatown needed no moon to light its streets. Jackson found them ever the same. Some people recognized him, gave him nods of courtesy and an ever-wide berth. He supposed this helped him find the small room above a restaurant leaking the scents of bao and soy from every crevice. He supposed he didn't care. What he cared for was the hand in his suitcase, the fire escape outside his window, and the shadowed figure he imagined there through the night.

Morning came and with it the racket below. He wondered if the streets were ever quiet, and didn't mind that they weren't. He stood at the window and watched the way the people moved, the business they conducted. There was a bookstore across the street beside a vegetable market. A short way down, there was the place with gleaming ducks in the window. Jackson liked to count them; this morning, there were seventeen. He counted them twice in an effort to distract himself from the pain in his hands. It didn't work. He tried to shift forms, but couldn't get there, either; the pain was too much, all consuming.

Before the sun could creep over the buildings, he left his room, taking a good five minutes to lock the door on his way out. His hands were near useless, the pain blinding, and the key was so small. He drew deeper into his coat as he left, taking to the alleys he knew so well. The den was easily found, if not by its shadowed doorway then by the sweet scent that bled down the length of the alleyway. He didn't care that the room was already busy, these men likely having spent the evening in the dragon's embrace. He cared that this smoke would take the pain away, that for a little while he would be able to escape what Cressida had done to him.

They knew him here, but only as enforcer, not habitué. He was welcomed, the old Chinese men making low sounds in their throats when they noticed the wreck of his hands. They could be mended, they told him. Jackson shook them off, he wanted only the bliss of opium, wanted only this corner pallet and to be undisturbed.

At first, he couldn't hold the pipe himself, for the weight of it was agony in his hands. He snarled when the men offered their help; they wanted only to please, but he kicked them away, turned his shoulder to the wall, and found a way he could brace the pipe against his arm, against his knee, against anything that was not his fucking hand. He passed the morning this way, waking to the evening lanterns being lit, his body pleasantly numb.

He paid them in gold, more than they asked. They drew a divider around his pallet so he might have privacy in his agony, but there were hours spent sobbing, and this unnerved the others in the rooms. None ever asked what was wrong with him; they did not need to know, for they came with their own problems. As he did not ask of them (could not, for he was not aware of anything in those hours), they afforded him the same perceived kindness.

Once, he thought Foster came. Later, he would tell himself it was ridiculous, but there were times he believed his familiar weight rested on his pallet, those wrinkled hands smelling of metal stroking his hair back from his sweaty face. He would have sworn it was Foster who tied him down and bent his fingers back into reasonable shapes even while Jackson screamed down the sky.

He woke another time, arms tied down, the mouth of the pipe against his own. He drew a long draught of the smoke, feeling as though he were wrapped in cotton. If he looked past the wreath of smoke, there were lions peering down at him, blinking their large eyes, yawning their even larger mouths. When they turned, they were only paper, sliver-thin as they padded across the room and away.

There was food — bao torn into small pieces, slipped into his mouth by fingers terribly familiar (soft, so soft, yet on some of the edges, calloused from using a whip). There was tea, sharp and green against his tongue in a cup as wide as the ocean. There were other things he could not name, all softly edged, smudged and running like ink in water. They passed in and out of his awareness like a dream, things he could not hold even if he possessed hands.

His hands and the world came back to him slowly. When at last he could sit up and look around, he was disgusted with himself, called himself a coward, a fool, which the Chinese men agreed with. Slow nods, but they offered more tea, showed him where clean clothes awaited him, and helped him dress. These clothes reminded him of those Foster wore, roomy and easily tied shut, for his fingers could not manage buttons. He wondered if they ever would again.

The room he had taken above the restaurant was another world. His suitcase was there, untouched, and as the sky opened with rain, Jackson watched the patterns the water made through the window onto the lid of the metal box containing Sister Jerome Grace's hand.

What had become of the rest of her?

He opened the box, slow and torturous work with his healing hands. He sat cross-legged at the foot of the bed, watching the rain play over that hand, its curled fingers. The sky played with the cross, brightening and darkening it by turns. Shadows crept into the palm and then out. And always, the threads of life poured from the severed end.

Jackson touched them only once. He expected them to be cold, but they ran with warmth. Cressida had meant to kill the sister. Judging by the hand, it didn't seem she had succeeded. The threads spiraled around his fingers as gentle as air; perhaps they had more presence, but Jackson could not feel it, not beyond the low lick of constant pain.

Mae did not come to him, so he went to her. It took days by the method he chose. He went over the roofs, quickly discovering he wasn't yet well enough to do it. How simple the streets would have been.

He called himself a fool, but wanted to master the roofs again, wanted to force his body into it. His hands no longer gripped the fire escape rails well, nor the gutters. He had also never taken the roofs from this deep inside Chinatown, so finding a path was one of the first challenges.

When at last he did, the accomplishment rested warm around his shoulders. It took too much time, but night after night, Jackson grew more adept at travelling this way, hands regaining their strength as he found the path north to Bell's.

Bell's remained a flood of light amid the city, people flocking to its graceful theater. On the surface, nothing had changed. The massive gargoyles remained at their posts. Jackson wound farther north, to the back of the building, where he could leap across and crouch on the roof. He imagined he could feel the music in the stones. He imagined Mae on the stage, the desire of every man in the room, though she wanted none of them, would allow none of them. Imagined her mouth on his, dark and soft, and —

He was in the theater before he realized he had gone. Had climbed down all those fire escapes to hit the street, pay his coin. His heart was a foolish bastard he thought, but he didn't care, because in this room were things better than opium, better than fizzing soda.

When Mae strode onto the stage, something had changed. Whether it was within her, or within him, he wasn't sure, but he could see into her in a way he hadn't before. Threads coursed through her, from head to toe and back again. They reached through the floor and ceiling both, but none of them anchored her. She moved without restriction, like air or water, going where she would. And then the light shifted and these threads vanished as if they had never been. Jackson almost sensed their weight inside himself, but refused the idea as ridiculous.

Playfully the lions mauled Mae and she vanished into the understage. The lions knew their place; they turned on the audience, to roar as if they meant to eat them too. Everyone leaped back, gasped, and fear only turned to delight when the lions padded away. As they did so, Jackson slipped backstage, down the stairs with the lions who regarded him with solemn eyes. The carousel girls were back, flooding the stage in the lions' wake.

One lion moved toward Jackson and his heart caught. The beast lifted its head, taking a long smell of Jackson. As if it could smell the months spent in the opium den, the lion's nose wrinkled. It gave him a gentle nudge, granting permission. Jackson caught the edge of the understage door with his boot and eased it open enough to slip inside where Mae crouched on the thin mattress. She didn't move.

"Did you go out of guilt?"

Her question surprised him. It spurred him into motion, until he kneeled with her on the mattress. He didn't touch her, not because his hands ached — some part of him knew they always would — but because she was not entirely his. Arrogant, that. No person belonged to any other person — people were as changeable as the weather. But when at last Mae did move, she lifted her head and pinned him with her black gaze and he knew, knew the way he knew so much else he couldn't explain, that she was his and he was hers, as much as they could be.

He laughed, a ragged sound. "Not a shred of guilt," he said. It was a simple admission, but lifted something from his shoulders. He should have felt guilty, for Cressida hadn't been a stranger at a sideshow. She was known to him, had clothed him and fed him and took him in when no other family would. She had dared him to believe in himself and he had killed her.

"Would have swallowed her had you and Beth not come," he said. "Is easy to say …" He exhaled, not looking from her eyes. "She meant to kill Foster. She broke my fingers. She used all of us to further her own ends, but … Everyone does." He reached for her now, one crooked finger whispering over a curl of hair. "Lachesis."

At the sound of her true name, she came apart. Jackson thought he had killed her too, but the sweetest pleasure he had ever seen crossed her face a split second before she dissolved and then …

Thread, everywhere thread. She spilled until she filled the understage, until Jackson could swim in the mass of them. He pushed his aching hands through the threads and knew her hum with a pleasure so fierce it flooded into the building and set it to shaking.

The harder he stroked the thread, the harder the world itself moved, skewed and off-balance, and when he gathered them in bunches and clumsily braided them together, she surged between his legs. She slid around his waist, throat, and across the open gap of his mouth.

It was a slow devouring, one in which his broken hands did not matter. Mae rose up through these threads, keeping coiled tight around him. Jackson drew a breath and let himself fall apart the way she had. Her eyes were black and on him and she did not look away.

AUTHOR BIO

E. Catherine Tobler has never run away to join the circus — but she thinks about doing so every day. Among others, her short fiction has appeared in *Clarkesworld*, *Lightspeed*, and on the Theodore Sturgeon Memorial Award ballot. Her first novel, *Rings of Anubis*, launched the Folley & Mallory Adventures. Senior editor of *Shimmer Magazine*, you can find her online at www.ecatherine.com and @ecthetwit.

ACKNOWLEDGMENTS

The idea for Jackson's Unreal Circus and Mobile Marmalade arrived during a winter where the snow piled itself up to the windowsills. I wanted to get away and started dreaming about trains cutting paths through tall snow, high grass, black tunnels. Of course they weren't ordinary trains.

Jackson was insistent from the first, if elusive — and I suspect he's cross with the revelations I've shared here. Jackson is the private kind, and was slow to tell his own story when there were so many others to share first. Others he found more worthy than his own.

My thanks to Ellen Datlow, who published the first traveling circus story I ever wrote in *SciFiction*, and to Scott H. Andrews, who published the most recent in *Beneath Ceaseless Skies*. To A.C. Wise, who always wanted a circus novel, and still dreams of a collection (me, too). To Beth Wodzinski, who never ceases to cheer my writing endeavors, no matter how weird they get. To my spoon-shaped muse, whom I cannot explain and could not do without.

This book stands alone, as do all other circus stories, but I hope that if you explore them as a whole, you will find something magical indeed.

APEX PUBLICATIONS NEWSLETTER

Why sign up?

Newsletter-only promotions. Book release announcements. Event invitations. And much, much more!

If you choose to sign up for the Apex Publications newsletter, we will send you an email confirmation to insure that you in fact requested the newsletter and to avoid unwanted emails. Your email address is always kept confidential, and we will only use it to send you newsletters or special announcements. You may unsubscribe at any time, and details on how to unsubscribe are included in every newsletter email.

Visit